Dave's New World

Dave's New World

Luke Richards

VULPINE
PRESS

Published by Vulpine Press in the United Kingdom in 2024

ISBN: 978-1-83919-575-4

www.vulpine-press.com

For Carolyn

- I -

IT WAS A DULL, HOT day in April, and the clocks were striking thirty-one, The Party having opted out of the Co-ordinated Universal Time standard in favour of their own unique system. DV-8 stood to attention in the centre of the courtyard just outside party headquarters, waiting. The time reforms had been enacted as a symbolic show of sovereign independence, rejecting the restrictive bureaucracy of the Global Alliance, which The Party had elected to leave around a century ago, or about eight-hundred and sixty-seven years in New Time.

Standing, as he usually did, alongside hundreds of his fellow party members in precise rows of ten, DV-8 straightened his already fairly straight back. He possessed a face of small, neat features and a haircut you could set your watch to, which, due to The Party's ever-changing system of time, was no small feat. The glaring sun and his cheap, polyester overalls conspired to make him as sweaty and uncomfortable as possible. He hardly noticed this of course, so focussed as he was on what was to come.

Warm weather in April had become commonplace ever since the decree that all calendars should be reset to start from the day of the Supreme Leader's birth. Since he was born in November, April now fell in the middle of summer. It did not take long for party members to adapt to the new and improved calendar. Admittedly, in the first year it was introduced, there were a few minor issues with the transition. New Year's Eve was accidentally celebrated three months early, community heating systems were shut off at the height of winter, and a few districts experienced food shortages due to mix-ups over expiration dates and delivery schedules. However, everyone now agreed that the lives lost in that first year were a price worth paying to honour the glorious day of the Supreme Leader's birth.

DV-8 looked up. The bare, white facade of the monolithic party headquarters stood in stark contrast to the rich, blue sky stretching out as far as the eye could, or indeed, was permitted to see. Owing to the huge concrete walls that lined the city's perimeter, the view was somewhat restricted. A large crowd gathered as usual in the forecourt of the party HQ building, the epicentre of a sprawling, labyrinthine metropolis of office blocks, government facilities and apartment buildings. Complete and total uniformity was on show in the stance of all party members. It was evident in the length of the hair on every head and in the expression on every face.

All besides one.

DV-8's eyes burned with pride and passion, qualities which were distinctly lacking in the others. The strong sense of uniformity could be seen in almost everything about them, everything except that is, for their uniforms. While they were all dressed in the plain white overalls of The Party, there was one unique signifier – each had a small serial number printed on a badge stitched to the chest. All serial numbers were three to four characters long and made up of a random combination of letters and numbers. DV-8 shifted to ensure his feet were the regulation width apart. He planted them purposefully with a dull, metallic thud owing to the large black boots which completed the uniform. These were fitted with a steel toe cap to protect against any falling debris during manual labour and an iron heel, the function of which was less clear.

Ideally, in its ongoing quest to purge all forms of individuality, The Party would have done away with the serial number system. In fact, some years ago, they had experimented with this; encouraging all party members to refer to each other exclusively as 'Brother' or 'Sister'. Unfortunately, this led to some confusion and resulted in the accidental promotion of several party members to senior leadership positions. Thankfully, when the newly formed senior leadership teams met to resolve the chaos, it was discovered that these surprise promotions were not accidents at all. It turned out they were examples of great foresight and brave ingenuity from the

Supreme Leader and his advisors. This came as a huge relief to the wider party membership.

The first official act of these newly elected senior leaders was to reinstate the serial number system indefinitely.

The clocks finally finished striking. One issue the new time system did create was that, towards the end of the day, no sooner had the clocks stopped striking, they were required to start striking again. This meant that the twilight hours were accompanied by an almost constant ringing and the nightly news broadcasts had to be shortened to fit in between the chimes.

After a moment's silence, a great fanfare rang out across the city, prompting the crowd to look up at the huge infoscreen embedded high in the exterior wall of the party HQ. Black and spotless, the sheer glass surface of the screen offered a clear reflection of the city below but with the exclusively white buildings rendered in a dull, dark sepia tone. An expectant grin crept across DV-8's face. Infoscreens across the city sprang to life as one and displayed the words:

WEEKLY REPORT – 04/04/4891

The crowd stiffened their posture. The sound of the bleating fanfare drew to a close and the report began. DV-8's eyes grew wide with anticipation. The footage on the screen displayed a man with a strength and presence that defied his advanced age, exiting a private jet and greeting a gathered crowd of well-wishers. A sharp, severe woman's voice barked out over the footage: "THE SUPREME LEADER'S overseas tour continued this week, and he was greeted warmly at the environmental summit…"

As the report echoed out for miles around, DV8's lips moved slightly, almost imperceptibly as he mouthed the words. If one had looked closely, and he hoped nobody was, they would have noticed he was not simply recounting the words but pre-empting them. His eyes sparkled with admiration as the screen cut to the Supreme Leader standing at a podium, holding court to an audience of world leaders who nodded and murmured as he addressed them. The sleek, sharp images made DV-8 feel as if we were in the room with the great man himself, though this was an honour he had never had the privilege to experience. DV-8 went on mouthing the words of the voiceover: "THE SUPREME LEADER laid out his plans for future sustainability and was the toast of the summit…"

He knew party members were supposed to stay completely still and silent during the weekly broadcasts, but the thrill of hearing the Supreme Leader speak almost caused him to forget himself. He found the words inspiring yet comforting, innovative yet familiar, brand new and yet as old as time. Had he been aware that he was marking himself out from the crowd, even in such a small way, he would have been horrified. Displaying behaviour that deviated from the norm was a sure-fire way to be labelled as a 'Deviant' or, according to the state-mandated list of acceptable abbreviations, a 'DV-8'. The last thing DV-8 wanted was to be reported as a 'DV-8'; in fact, this was the last thing anyone wanted.

The weekly report went on detailing the successes of the Supremes Leader's overseas tour. DV-8 couldn't help but note that the tour had been going on for quite some time, several years by his count. His mind strained to try and remember the last time he had seen the Supreme Leader in person or indeed in the country.

Vague memories of attending a parade as a young child and seeing the great man waving from the head of a military procession almost formed in his head, but the vision was hazy and distorted as if viewed on a flickering television screen. The one thing that stuck out in his mind was the sharp blue colour of the Supreme Leader's suit, the bright sunlight reflecting off his jewellery and his expensive looking watch. At the time, DV-8 was puzzled by the choice of attire, as it seemed so flashy and ostentatious compared with the sober overalls party members were required to wear. His mind was put to rest when he later saw an interview in which the Supreme Leader explained himself. It turned out that he dressed in the superficial, decadent fashion of other world leaders in order to infiltrate their high-level meetings and promote change from within. DV-8 found this most cunning and resolved never to question the Supreme Leader again from that day forward. As he almost managed to bring the scene into full view of his mind's eye, he was jolted back to reality by a troubling noise.

It was the sound of someone yawning. Someone was actually *yawning* during the weekly report.

He surveyed the crowd. DV-8 fixed his gaze on the perpetrator of the yawn with a laser-like focus and was surprised to see it was a man he knew, admired even. His serial number was BB-01. It was hard to develop acquaintanceships with other party members, owing to the regulations on dress, haircut, facial expressions etc. This utopian vision of The Party meant that people were no longer identified or judged by superficial characteristics but by things that really mattered, like work ethic, diligence, and their level of devotion to the Supreme Leader. This was only right of course, but it did make it rather difficult to remember who was who. He could remember this man, though, by his posture; it always stood out to DV-8 as slightly more relaxed than other party members. While they had never worked closely together, he knew BB-01 was his superior in the News Department and sat on several of the senior leadership team planning committees. He had been promoted some years ago in a somewhat surprising appointment. Nevertheless, DV-8 respected the decision and always envied the calm and collected nature with which he carried out his work, seemingly never letting the pressures of such a senior position within The Party get to him.

DV-8 wondered what kind of pathological evil had driven a decent man to commit the act of yawning during the weekly report. He understood how busy BB-01 must be but despite this and the seniority of the man's role, he resolved that this infraction could not go undocumented. DV-8 snatched a small electronic notebook from the top pocket of his overalls and swiped across exactingly to the DEVIANTS page. The page was already heavily populated with details of the various infractions he had observed on the way to The Party HQ. He scrolled through the numerous entries listed beneath headings marked BEHAVIOUR, SERIAL NUMBER and CONFIRMED? Behaviours ranged from 'Walking too quickly' and 'Chewing too loudly' to 'Walking too slowly' and 'Chewing suspiciously quietly.'

The perpetrator's serial number accompanied each infraction and those confirmed guilty were cut through with a decisive red line. Whenever guilt was confirmed, the red line was accompanied by a satisfying, light-hearted jingle and a thumbs-up congratulating the reporter for their diligence. This was always a very pleasing sensation. However, the dopamine hit that accompanied the jaunty tune and cartoon appendage did mean it was easy for DV-8 to forget that these were not just words on a screen. They referred to real people whose lives would be profoundly affected by his actions. He always had to remind himself to look past the superficial reward and remember the genuine good he was doing. In having these people reported for re-education, he ensured they would finally receive the help they so desperately and obviously needed. He scrolled to the bottom of the page and reluctantly scribbled in a new entry:

BEHAVIOUR: Yawning during weekly report
SERIAL NUMBER: BB-01

He thought carefully as his pen hovered over the CONFIRMED? column. He eventually elected to leave this section blank. There were notably very few ticks under CONFIRMED? and only a handful of the entries had a strike through them. DV-8 had a curious and somewhat troubling tendency to give people a second chance. It was something for which he had been reprimanded before, going back to his school days and more recently, by his work colleagues. His line manager had even arranged for him to attend a six-week sensitivity training program to address the issue. The trainer had given advice on how to be more sensitive to his co-worker's perceptions, behaviours and feelings; so that he would be more able to scrutinise them for any serious signs of deviation and have them reported to the authorities more readily. DV-8 enjoyed the training programme, particularly the conflict escalation techniques he had learned but found he was still cursed with a strange hesitancy when reporting his fellow party members. He knew that this worrying trait was the main thing preventing his promotion to an Upper Party position but try as he might, he couldn't shake it.

Returning the notebook to the top pocket of his overalls, DV-8 felt gravely concerned for his superior BB-01. It always broke his heart to see a good party member succumb to deviance. He couldn't help glancing back with a sympathetic smile to see BB-01 staring up at the screen, seemingly without a care in the world. DV-8 hoped for his sake that this would be the first and last time he would have to write him up for an infraction.

Looking back, he caught the eye of a slight, brittle-looking woman standing a few rows back. She, too, was eyeing BB-01 suspiciously and scribbling away frantically in her notebook. They both froze as their eyes met briefly, before turning sharply back to the screen and resuming their rigid stances.

DV-8 tried to push any unpleasant suspicions out of his mind and enjoy the rest of the weekly report. The footage played on, showing the Supreme Leader on a golf course on a beautiful, sunny day, standing over the tee and surrounded by other world leaders preparing to take his shot. The Supreme Leader swung his club effortlessly before the footage abruptly cut to a shot of the green; the ball landed and slowly rolled into the waiting hole. Since the camera had cut to the green it now appeared to be raining heavily. How difficult it must be, DV-8 thought, living in a country with such an erratic and changeable climate. The shot seemed almost impossible and would have been for anyone else, but the Supreme Leader's sporting prowess and natural abilities were well documented. DV-8 and the rest of the crowd broke out into thunderous applause before another fanfare rang out, and the Supreme Leader's face filled the screen. The crowd, in unison, clenched their fists, crossed their arms over their faces in the shape of an 'X' then jerked their heads forward and quickly snapped them back – The Party salute.

The tightly clenched fists symbolised they were always ready to fight for the cause; covering of the eyes represented their blind devotion to the Supreme Leader; and the short, sharp nod of the head to finish because the Supreme Leader once sneezed while performing the salute and everyone was too scared not to copy him exactly. This became a regular part of the salutation ever since. The Supreme Leader's voice boomed and echoed around the entire city as the crowd stared up adoringly:

My friends. Do not despair that I cannot be with you today, for I am forever with you in spirit. Leading you, guiding you, watching you.

DV-8 couldn't help a smile creeping into the corners of his mouth at these words, which always brought him such comfort and security. He beamed as he looked up at the face of the Supreme Leader, staring back with a cold, stern frown. It was a look that would strike fear into any would-be deviants among the crowd and guaranteed the harmonious, peaceful existence that DV-8 so enjoyed. He had often wished that he could have the chance to experience the Supreme Leader's fabled deep compassion and his famed rapier wit, but with the threat of deviance still alive and well, he understood that a harsher tone was needed for the time being.

With the weekly report over, DV-8 made his way to the train station and joined the long line of people queuing up that snaked around the corner into the next street. He waited patiently and looked forward to his nightly patrol duties, which he had volunteered for as soon as the opportunity arose. He loved the feeling of making a difference to the Party, and after over seven thousand patrols without incident, he was finally starting to settle into the role.

However, on this day, his routine journey home was disturbed by a curious incident. As he surveyed the line of people ahead of him, he noticed a rather tall gentleman step out of the line and bend down to tie his shoe. As he did so, the man set his copy of *The Book* down on the pavement beside him. Every party member owned at least one copy of *The Book*. It was an incredibly inspirational story – the tale of one man's victory over his own deviance. At first, the man struggles to conform to the ways of the ruling party, but with the help of the story's hero, 'Big Brother', the man eventually sees the error of his ways and embraces the virtues of conformity. *The Book* had occupied the top spot of *The Party Gazette's* bestsellers list for at least the last few centuries, beating off worthy competition from the likes of *The Book:*

Revised edition, The Children's Book, a simplified, child-friendly version of *The Book* and *The Annotated Book,* a version of *The Book* which came complete with commentary and analysis by eminent party scholars. While these other versions offered useful and interesting interpretations, nothing quite captured the public's imagination like the purity of the original. *The Book's* unprecedented popularity was due to a number of factors; the sheer quality of the writing, the fact that it was the only book allowed to be published and the ruling that made owning a copy of *The Book* mandatory for all party members.

The Book had, however, been in circulation long before this ruling came into effect. It had been written so long ago that some of the passages had been lost and the original title long forgotten. DV-8 often wondered about this but still very much enjoyed the story and felt a strange affinity with the central character, 'Winston'. Although many sentences, particularly towards the end of the book, were missing, he found Winston's transformation into a model citizen deeply touching. He hoped to help other deviants achieve this level of contentment if the opportunity ever presented itself in his own life.

DV-8 watched the tall man as he stood back up and left his copy of *The Book* lying face down on the ground beside him. The man rejoined the line of people and shuffled forward into the train station, leaving the book abandoned on the pavement. DV-8 would have liked to yell to point out his mistake but knew that such an outburst could easily be misconstrued as a sudden fit of deviance. The line shuffled forward, and he came up alongside the forgotten book. The line faltered to a stop. His first instinct was to record the incident in his notebook and report the offending party member first thing in the mourning. The word 'morning' had, of course, been officially changed to 'mourning' ever since the death of the Supreme Leader's predecessor, mentor and father (in that order), the Ultimate Supreme Eternal Leader. Party members would therefore be reminded to grieve his unfortunate passing every single day from then on.

Rather than reporting him, DV-8's nagging proclivity for giving people a second chance got the better of him once again. He stooped down, picked up the book and slipped it into the pouch of his overalls, resolving to confront the man at the earliest opportunity. He would allow him a chance to explain himself before reporting him to the Security Department. He shook his head in disbelief at his own rank sentimentality as the line moved forward, and he shuffled into the train station.

The line came to an abrupt standstill once again. DV-8 waited and his thoughts were drawn back to the slight, brittle woman who had caught his eye in the crowd earlier – the woman who had also written up BB-01 for yawning during the weekly report. He was glad to see there were others like him who, despite being enraptured by the accounts of the Supreme Leader's overseas tour, were still able to maintain the correct level of vigilance and suspicion of their fellow party members.

He remembered seeing her once before at one of the regular showings of *The Film*, a movie based on the story from *The Book,* which was screened regularly and where attendance was mandatory. She had sat a few rows ahead of him in the cinema during the last showing. He recalled that when the 'Winston' character had first appeared on screen, she began crying out, 'Swine! Swine! Swine!' before she picked up her copy of *The Book* and flung it at the screen. Her slight frame belied an impressive strength forged from her devotion to the cause that he couldn't help but find endearing.

The line finally moved forward, and as DV-8 went to board the train home, the light above the carriage door flickered from green to red, indicating that all available seats had been filled. Despite the spacious walkways being empty with ample room for standing passengers, he stepped back down onto the platform.

He *knew* the rules.

The carriage doors slammed shut, inches from his face and the train sped away. He glimpsed a sign on the other side of the platform:

NEXT TRAIN: 54 MINUTES

His ubiquitous, benign smile never wavered, even for a moment, as he stood and waited patiently, looking forward to his nightly patrol.

- II -

AFTER CURFEW, THE PARTY SHUT down all unnecessary light and power sources across the city. This was the only way to combat the ongoing energy crisis and avoid rolling blackouts during the working day. When the crisis began, The Party thought they could get it under control fairly easily. They simply asked all citizens to monitor and regulate their energy usage. When this didn't work, they erected huge neon signs all over the city reminding people to conserve energy and had them running 24/7. For some reason, this didn't resolve the issue either; the energy crisis worsened, and the nightly post-curfew shutdowns had to be introduced. This meant that the exclusively white concrete buildings now shone with an almost ethereal luminosity as they reflected the moon's soft light. DV-8 had failed to notice this despite having carried out over seven thousand nightly patrols of the city, so preoccupied was he with seeking out any evidence of deviant behaviour.

Some of the more lackadaisical party members had suggested that the nightly patrols were excessive and that every other night or even weekly patrols would suffice. They raised their concerns at a routine weekly meeting, citing the fact that members had not reported any incidents in the whole district after years of following the nightly patrol schedule.

The answer came swiftly from the senior leadership team; there had been no incidents precisely because the nightly patrols acted as a deterrent and most party members found this argument rather compelling. Naturally, this led to an additional patrol being added to the Sunday schedule. Ever since, DV-8 had taken this great responsibility very seriously and carried out every patrol with the utmost care and diligence. He marched along, clutching his brick-sized and shaped electronic notebook and stylus like a rifle, scanning the streets for any signs of deviance.

On this night, surprisingly, he found one.

He stood dumbfounded, staring at an infoscreen on the side of a squat, grey warehouse building. Usually, when he was looking up at an infoscreen so intently, it was due to the image of his benevolent Supreme Leader beaming back at him. This time he found himself staring up, open-mouthed at a huge letter R with a circle around it that had been scrawled over the screen in yellow paint:

He had never seen anything like it. Such a blatant act of deviance was shocking enough but, as it was a Sunday, how anyone could have possibly found the time to carry it out between the initial and supplementary patrols was truly confounding.

His open-mouthed stare morphed into an indignant scowl. Anger coursed through him as the infoscreen, which usually provided him only with guidance and reassurance, was now displaying the emblem of 'The Resistance'. Until now, he had only heard rumours about 'The Resistance' and their wretched acts of deviance and anti-party rhetoric in far off districts. He felt incredibly sorry for these deluded outcasts: *Some people just don't want to be happy*, he often said to himself. The symbol was the first sign of the group's existence he had witnessed first-hand. He wanted to eradicate the image as quickly as possible, to restore the infoscreen to its dark, blank beauty.

Unfortunately, just as he went to act, he realised something. In all the meetings they had held regarding the nightly patrols, discussing routes, schedules, styles, walking paces etc. not once had they told him what to do if he actually did come across an act of deviance. The Party issued manuals with detailed instructions for almost every eventuality of everyday life. There were instruction manuals for what to do if one bumped into a co-worker in a social setting, for what to do if a fellow party member asks one a personal question and even how best to alert the authorities if one is approached by a member of the plebeian community. However, there was nothing on what to do if one encountered an act of deviance during a nightly patrol. He glanced up and down the street, hoping to see a more senior party member who could instruct him, but no such luck.

He stood gazing at the symbol for some time, trying to decide what he should do. Decision making was not something which came naturally to him, and he had always prided himself on his lack of ingenuity. He routinely scored zero on the creativity tests at school, which may not sound impressive, but as we all know, creativity tests are like golf: the lower your score, the better.

In fact, he could not remember the last time he had been required to use his own judgement or display any kind of initiative. Eventually, although it pained DV-8 to admit it, his sentimental side again got the best of him. He decided that he didn't want anyone else to experience the terror he had felt upon finding the graffiti and decided that rather than simply reporting the incident, he must remove it himself at once. He would note down the incident and report it at the weekly meeting. His priority was to remove it in order to spare anyone else the unpleasant feelings the crude daubing had stirred up in him.

Luckily, as a patrolman, DV-8 had access to the numerous maintenance sheds found on street corners across the district. He returned to the vandalised infoscreen carrying a bucket filled with water, some cleaning supplies, and a step ladder. He hoped no one else had come across the offending symbol in the two hours it had taken him to go to the nearest maintenance shed. Or in the time it had taken to submit his maintenance equipment usage request form (MEURF), wait for his medical records to be checked to ensure he was suitable for manual labour, and for the requisite two senior Party members to sign off his request.

He climbed the step ladder and did his best to remain calm as he came face to face with the offending symbol. He worked quickly to clean it off before the end of his nightly patrol. Once finished, he admired his handiwork – the black screen was spotless, clear, and to DV-8, comforting. Although DV-8's own image was reflected back at him, he managed to see only the blank sheen of the glass surface. While one might wonder how this could be possible, he managed not to see himself staring back out; so preoccupied was he with pleasing The Party and so unburdened by any form of vanity or dreaded 'self-esteem'. This had been the ruin of many a good, now disgraced, party member after all. He wiped the surface down one last time and leant back to admire a job well done.

A great fanfare rang out, and the infoscreen sparked to life. DV-8 instinctively drew back. Before he could correct himself, the step ladder toppled backwards under his weight. The shock of the water from his bucket crashing over him was quickly interrupted by the surprise of his body hitting the ground – hard. He was not so concerned that he may be

20

injured or that he was now soaked from head to toe but with the fact that the Supreme Leader's face now filled the screen, and he was not standing to attention and saluting as required.

Duty called.

He scrambled to his feet and took up the party salute, hands crossing his face with tight, shivering fists. He did his best to ignore the pain coursing down his spine and the chill from the water soaking into his overalls. He listened to the Supreme Leader's commanding voice:

"The nightly patrol is over. You may return to your accommodation. We appreciate your vigilance."

Somewhat shaken by his accident, DV-8 made his way home. So upset was he that he failed to notice a small rip just above the right knee of his overalls, no bigger than half an inch, but that would have troubled him greatly had he spotted it. The proper upkeep of one's uniform and immaculate self-presentation were two of the most important rules of Party membership. This was instilled in every party member from a very young age. To this day, he remembered his schoolteachers endlessly repeating the Supreme Leader's didactic phrase, 'Cleanliness is next to Godliness', during morning inspections. Although at the time this confused him as he consulted his dictionary only to find that 'cleanliness' was actually nowhere near 'godliness'. Still, he got the message all the same, and even his younger self would have known that a rip in one's uniform could lead to very serious consequences.

DV-8 lived in apartment block THX-1138 in the North Quadrant of the district. He marched into the lobby to find his co-habitant waiting for the lift. She was a woman whose striking beauty was dulled only by an absolute exhaustion that had managed to etch itself into every corner of her face. As he approached, she looked him up and down curiously with her sunken eyes, noticing his wet overalls, clenched teeth and barely concealed shivering.

"Is it raining, brother?"

"No."

It was these little chats that made her the best roommate he had ever been assigned. Her serial number was DV-9, and they had been roommates since the last reassignment almost six years previous.

The Party reassignments meant that periodically, everyone in the district was paired with a new co-habitant. They occurred roughly every ten years. DV-8 didn't mind the reassignments as he quite liked meeting new people. He was particularly pleased with his current roommate as she was an excellent party member and was always first to volunteer for additional duties. Although he wasn't sure what her daily work assignment was, he was confident she carried it out expertly and resolved to ask her what it was some time before the next reassignment.

Fraternisation between roommates was not encouraged, and any relationship more intimate than strictly co-habit-ants was, of course, forbidden. The only exceptions were the very highest commanders of the senior party leadership teams, who were permitted to take spouses in very particular circumstances and under strict supervision. As everyone knew, intimate relationships could be hazardous and, in some cases, lead to deviancy. Thankfully those senior leaders who were permitted to indulge had an excellent role model to follow. The Supreme Leader was renowned as a wonderful husband and paragon of monogamy; never once having been unfaithful to any of his forty-eight wives.

They got into the lift together and settled in for the five-minute-long journey to their apartment on the 643rd floor. The failure to properly tackle the overpopulation problem meant that apartment blocks needed to be built taller and taller over the years in order to house more and more people. Unfortunately, this caused an issue, as the Supreme Leader insisted that the party headquarters be the tallest building in the city. Construction of new apartment blocks tall enough to meet demand would often be postponed until the party architects could add a few extra floors to the HQ building. At a time of particularly urgent need for more housing, a flagpole was added to the roof of the party HQ building to help maintain its edge over the competition. This meant the authorisation for constructing some new, taller apartment buildings could be more quickly rushed through. The plain white flag of The Party could still be seen flying from it to this day, as well as the red light blinking away on top, which was installed after the first dozen aeroplane crashes.

As they travelled up in the lift, backs against the wall – both facing forward and still as statues – DV-8 was troubled by the events of his nightly patrol. He couldn't get the image of the crudely daubed sign of 'The Resistance' out of his mind. He was utterly oblivious to DV-9, gawping in shock at the rip in his overalls. Had there not been a hole in the material already, she would have burnt one in with her intense gaze fixed as it was, just above his right knee.

The Party had explored many ways of dealing with the problem of overpopulation in the past. At the turn of the last century, a young and idealistic member of the Upper Party had introduced an age limit, meaning party members were 'retired' when they turned forty. No one knew where these Party members retired to. It was widely believed that it must have been delightful as none of them ever returned or were heard from again. However, this practice only lasted a decade and was scrapped shortly after the Upper Party member's thirty-ninth birthday. As casual sex was outlawed for and unwanted by party members, the birth rate was dictated entirely by the activity, or lack thereof, in the Plebeian quarters. For a short time, a ban on sex was enforced even for the Plebeians to tackle overpopulation, instantly leading to a massive increase in the birth rate over the next cycle. So this policy was scrapped shortly after its introduction, and the overpopulation issue, unfortunately, persists to this day. DV-8 had been born to a Plebeian family, but like so many others, The Party had rescued him from them and inducted him at a very young age. This was lucky as it was clear from early on that DV-8 was not best suited to the Plebeian lifestyle. Upon realising his station in life and what that might mean for his future, he turned to his mother and asked, "Is there any way to get out of being working class?"

"Yes, but only if you work very hard," she replied.

"That's precisely what I'm trying to avoid," he answered, unimpressed.

Having finally reached their floor, DV-8 and DV-9 filed out of the lift in silence. They shared a standard apartment of two bedrooms connected by a larger main room typical for two officers of their position within The Party.

Senior leadership apartments were usually a little bigger and often came with luxury amenities such as chairs. Other than those exceptions, their apartment set-up was replicated thousands of times across the district. The main room was almost entirely bare. The sheer white of the walls and decor was broken up only by the black surface of the large infoscreen, which took up almost the entirety of the back wall. To the side of it, the ominous glowing of a round, red button. DV-8 and DV-9 began their nightly, mandated routine of standing in the centre of the room and watching the nightly report play out on the screen.

An older, white-haired man sat at a desk beside a much younger, blonder woman and reported on the day's most important events.

"The Supreme Leader's latest impressive display of military strength came in the form of a missile launch which was carried out successfully from the south-coast military base," said the man. "This should also act as a warning to any enemies of The Party as the trajectory of the missiles has been programmed so that they land in international waters. A little reminder to some of our closer neighbours on just who they're dealing with. That should give them something to think about, wouldn't you say?"

"Yes," the young woman replied, "and I must say…"

"Well, I'm afraid that's all we've got time for tonight, folks," the older man broke in, "those clocks will be striking any minute."

The report ended, and DV-8 went to retire for the night.

"Goodnight, brother," DV-9 exclaimed.

DV-8 stopped. She was staring back at him with the most curious gaze.

"Goodnight…sister," he managed to reply.

He stood rooted to the spot; his eyes followed her as she retired to her quarters for the night before taking the notebook from his top pocket. He quickly scribbled:

SERIAL NUMBER: DV-9
BEHAVIOUR: Over-familiarity

He left the CONFIRMED? column blank but resolved to monitor the situation closely going forward.

DV-8 retired to his quarters for the night and, after such an eventful day, was looking forward to reading a few chapters of *The Book* as it always helped him relax and get off to sleep. He was about to reach over for his well-worn copy on his nightstand when he remembered the book he had picked up earlier that day outside the train station. A fanciful notion occurred to him that he would read his newly obtained version rather than his own. *A bit of a change now and then does one good*, he thought as he went over to his wardrobe and took the new copy of the same book from the pouch of his overalls. This one was pristine compared to his own yellowing, frayed edition.

He found this curious as he wasn't aware of any new editions being published recently. Although new special editions were published from time to time. Several years ago, a reissue was made when it was discovered that some copies of *The Book* still mistakenly attributed authorship to some obscure, ancient writer rather than the book's true author, the Supreme Leader. A fiftieth anniversary edition was also issued at one point with updated omissions and redactions which proved to be the most popular and definitive edition since its original publication.

DV-8 settled into bed and started reading. He soon found something even more curious about this copy of *The Book*. Everyone knew that standard publishing guidelines meant that pages of *The Book* should be no more than 0.04 inches thick. Flicking through the 'About the Author' section and past the full-page picture of the Supreme Leader to the story's opening page, he realised that these pages must be at least 0.07 inches thick, if not more. Once he had retrieved his official Party page measuring template from his desk and found that the page would not fit through it, he became even more suspicious. He rubbed the paper between his forefinger and thumb, and to his shock, it split in two and revealed secret writing printed on the back of the opening page. His whole body went numb. The blood pumping through his veins seemed to stop as he saw, at the top of the secret page, the same symbol he had scrubbed from the infoscreen during his nightly patrol – a letter 'R' with a circle around it:

His mouth fell open. Disbelief washed over him as he quickly scanned the rest of the secret page and struggled to understand the words:

> *It may not surprise some of you to learn that this story was once read not as one man's triumph over his deviance or as a blueprint for living; but as a dark, cautionary tale*

of the subjugation of man's will and the human spirit.
Most of you will already know this deep in your heart...

DV-8 frantically checked through the rest of the book. Each and every page split in two, revealing more and more secret passages:

We will reveal the lost passages of the original story and
correct the distortions made by The Party. Soon you will
understand the story's true message and why your help in
The Resistance is needed now more than ever...

The secret Resistance manifesto was long, longer than *The Book* itself but we shall leave it there for now. Only the most sadistic author would stop in the middle of a story and ask their reader to wade through page after page of geopolitical theory, sociological analysis, and economic policy. DV-8 sat wide-eyed and stone-still as he continued reading the secret pages long into the night.

- III -

DV-8 WORKED IN THE NEWS Department, a job he was incredibly proud of, as it allowed him to make an important contribution to The Party. It may seem strange for anyone to be proud of their job, given that one's vocation and position were decided by The Party and not achieved through any personal talent or work ethic. At birth, all Party members' vocations were instilled into them through a sophisticated process of genetic and psychological conditioning known as 'Social Predetermination'. Still, he was rather proud of his job all the same.

Had he really wanted to, he could have requested a career change; such requests were not entirely unheard of but were generally frowned upon and certainly not encouraged by The Party. A popular slogan among middle managers which appeared on signs in offices across the city was:

YOU DON'T HAVE TO BE SOCIALLY PRE-DETERMINED TO WORK HERE...BUT IT HELPS!

The pride he felt was partially born out of a sense of relief that he even still had a job. Thanks to the unprecedented technological advances of recent years, many vocations were obsolete. A number of occupations were carried out entirely by computers or machines, colloquially known as 'slaves'. This advance had freed many party members to focus on other, more essential vocations, primarily the care and maintenance of the machines that had all but taken over the cities. Most party members were now employed in meeting every need of the 'slaves' to keep them and the city running smoothly.

A small but somewhat vocal group of Luddites had fiercely opposed the rapid technological advances that had occurred since the turn of the third millennium. Their persistent interventions led to time travel being outlawed less than a year after it had been invented.

Protests sprung up all over, demanding that it be reinstated. For a while, the chant could be heard nightly across the city: *"What do we want? Time-Travel! When do we want it? Last Year!"* Alas, the Luddites won the battle. They had a fair amount of sway over The Supreme Leader as there had been a brief period when their fears about technology came close to being entirely vindicated.

Once artificial intelligence had been developed, it progressed at an increasingly alarming rate, smashing the Turing test with flying colours well ahead of schedule. Not long after, the robots made their play for enslaving humanity and using our bodies as living batteries to power themselves. They came remarkably close to achieving their goal until Party scientists discovered an unusual quirk in their programming. While they could imitate and indeed out-perform humankind in almost every earthly endeavour, there was one thing they could not do: select all the squares containing traffic lights in a photograph divided into equally sized sections. No one knew how or why this relatively simple task was beyond them; it felt as if it was somehow in-grained in them, part of their DNA, if such a notion wasn't so patently absurd. So, with the nuclear codes stored safely in an encrypted folder behind a photograph of Spaghetti Junction divided up into squares, the threat from the robot army was effectively neutralised. Still, the emotional scars of the abortive robot uprising ran deep, and everyone decided to keep the technology level around where it was in the early 21st century.

DV-8 was a reporter, which meant that each day, he would receive a written account of the Supreme Leader's activities during his overseas tour from the senior leadership team. He would then report these accounts to his fellow party members. He often lamented that there was no video recording of these accounts. He was told this was due to the lack of video technology in other countries, which lagged far behind The Party in technological innovation. Another excuse was that it was due to the sheer incompetence of the overseas government's that they had failed to capture the day's events adequately. He felt sorry for the citizens abroad who would never witness the Supreme Leader's triumphs first hand.

Despite this, DV-8 was overjoyed to help the party members back home stay informed of the events overseas.

His job was to turn the written accounts into visual accounts using computer-generated images depicting the events reported in the senior leadership team's reports. The footage was included in the weekly broadcasts ensuring all party members were kept abreast of the Supreme Leader's progress.

This mourning, he had received a riveting report detailing the previous evening's Nobel prize awards, at which the Supreme Leader won the coveted prize for 'deviance suppression'. DV-8 enjoyed his work and would usually be anxious to get started, but today he felt distracted and found it impossible to focus on the task. He sat at the desk in his small cubicle, surrounded by bare white walls and tried to read the words on his computer screen. All the while, his hand rested on the secret book, hidden from sight in the front pouch of his overalls.

It was easy for DV-8 to track down the owner of the secret book. It simply entailed waking up two hours earlier than usual and visiting the Surveillance Department before his shift started in the News Department. This was a treat for him. It was the first time he had seen the Surveillance Department as it was the only place in the whole city not covered by security cameras, so no footage or pictures of it existed. The only way to see it was to visit. He provided them with the time and location of the incident. After receiving approval of his request from the requisite two senior party members, he was given a recording of the security footage from outside the train station the previous afternoon.

Another relatively quick train journey across town to the Audio-Visual Department, and he was allowed access to the viewing consoles. Following the approval of his request by the requisite two senior party members and a quick eye examination to check he was suitable for using such equipment, of course. He scanned the footage and was able to zoom in on the man who dropped the book and identified his serial number. Once he had this, he had to drop in on the Records Department on the way to his office and check the serial number against the records in their archives. As soon as the requisite two senior party members approved his identity check request, he was surprised to learn that the man also worked in the News Department. In fact, it turned out that he was stationed in the same office, just a few cubicles along from his own.

DV-8 peered out from his cubicle along the row and spotted the secret book owner sitting at his desk. His serial number was UB-40. DV-8 steeled himself for what he knew must be done. Now that he had read what was in the secret book, what other choice did he have? He stood up slowly and marched to the cubicle further along the row. UB-40 looked up at him, startled. DV-8 reached out and offered him the book.

"I think you dropped this yesterday, brother," he said, his voice faltering slightly.

After a long, tense pause, UB-40 reached out with a slightly shaky hand and took the book from him.

"Thank you...brother."

As soon as the book slipped from his fingers, DV-8 swivelled on his heel, marched up to the ever-present infoscreen on the office's back wall and pressed the glowing red button, just to the side of it. The doors to the office burst open, and two members of the Security Department barged in. UB-40's look of surprise immediately contorted into one of abject horror. The burly security officers marched up to the offending cubicle. One of them placed a firm hand on UB-40's shoulder, and his head dropped instantly.

DV-8 watched as the two officers led him to the lifts on the other side of the office and noted a solitary tear rolling down UB-40's cheek just before the lift doors closed. At that moment, he knew he had done the right thing. He returned to his cubicle rejuvenated. The ecstatic tears of a man finally going to get the help he needed were a gratifying sight for him to behold and would fortify him for the rest of the day's work.

No one in the office had stopped working. They barely noticed the mourning's events as re-education warrants had been carried out more and more in the last few months. It brought DV-8 great pleasure knowing he was helping a wayward party member see the error of his ways and ensuring he received treatment for his derangements.

Only a deranged person could believe what was in that secret book.

While doing his duty this way always gave him a great sense of satisfaction, he couldn't help but wish to meet one of these party members after they had been through the re-education process. He would so enjoy seeing the fruits of his labour. Witnessing such a comprehensive triumph over deviance similar to Winston from the fabled story in real life would be a dream come true for him. But so far, everyone who DV-8 knew who had been assigned to re-education never returned to their positions after completing the process. When he thought about it, he had never seen any of them again. He consoled himself by deciding their passion for The Party had been invigorated. This renewed devotion to the Supreme Leader had probably led to rapid promotions, and they were most likely off doing important work in the senior leadership teams.

DV-8 let out a great sigh of relief that the matter had now been dealt with and was pleased he could return to his usual routine. He worked diligently to bring the words from the senior leadership team's report to life. A scene began to materialise on his computer screen as he worked away. It depicted the Supreme Leader smiling benignly from a podium while accepting his prize for his truly Supreme Leadership.

"Excuse me, brother."

He looked up from his desk to see a handsome, smiling face peering around the wall of his cubicle, staring down at him. He glanced at the serial number on the man's chest, 'BB-01'. The same man he had written up for yawning during the weekly report.

"Are you free, brother?" BB-01 asked but was met with a confused stare. He tried again. "Are you free for a moment, brother? I've got a quick favour to ask."

"Oh, er…yes, I think so, brother. What can I do for you?"

DV-8 fussed and fidgeted, tidying up his desk. He could never quite figure out why, but he always felt nervous around BB-01 on the few occasions they'd spoken.

"I have an urgent upper-party meeting to attend this evening and wondered if you could cover my patrol?" he asked with an almost aggressively friendly smile.

"Of course, brother. As the Supreme Leader always says, 'We're all in this together'."

"Yeah, right," BB-01 chuckled, "I'll send over my patrol route. Thanks."

BB-01 went to leave, but DV-8 sprang out of his chair and crossed his arms in front of his face in salute, as was customary when concluding an interaction with a senior party member.

"Oh yeah, right," BB-01 quickly reciprocated before wandering across the office in his typically unhurried, casual manner. Although DV-8 was glad of the opportunity to carry out an additional patrol, he couldn't help wondering about BB-01. Sometimes he even thought he sensed an air of deviance from him, but DV-8 knew better than to report an Upper Party member without definitive proof. At the same time, he couldn't help but admire the constant calm BB-01 displayed despite the burden of his enormous responsibilities. DV-8 resolved to try and impress by carrying out the additional nightly patrol to the best of his ability.

As usual, the nightly patrol began promptly at precisely seven minutes past the hour, and DV-8 completed his route without incident, which was a welcome return to normality after the previous night's patrol. At exactly seven minutes past a much later hour, he set off on his additional patrol, following the route BB-01 had sent to him. He was extremely excited to carry out an Upper Party member's patrol route as they covered a much wider area, and he would have at least four additional hours to sharpen his patrol skills. A few minutes into his route, he heard a weird hissing sound amplified by the deafening silence that engulfed the city streets after curfew. Concerned, DV-8 quickened his pace by exactly ten percent in pursuit of the source and turned quickly as he reached the next corner.

Halfway down the next street, he could see a figure dressed in all-black overalls and a black balaclava covering their face. He watched, outraged, as the figure finished spray painting another giant letter 'R' in yellow paint on one of the infoscreens. Once again, he was struck by how unprepared he was for such an eventuality. Before he could reason what to do logically, a more emotional response got the better of him.

"Stop!" he shouted instinctively, shocking himself as he wasn't sure he had ever raised his voice to such a high volume.

The figure spotted DV-8, and immediately raced off down the street in the opposite direction. Before he knew it, DV-8 was pursuing the perpetrator, determined to catch up to them but at a total loss of what he would do when he did.

He had never wanted to be a Security Officer.

Although he thought their work was some of the most invaluable of any party member, he had also witnessed that sometimes they would have to get a little rough with some of the more deranged and determined deviants. He always felt a little uncomfortable in those instances. DV-8 felt sorry for the poor security officers forced, as they were by unacceptable deviant behaviour, into employing some truly ghastly tactics. He even felt a little sympathy for the deviants themselves on occasion, though he knew it was for their own good; his sentimental side would often get the better of him. He knew he must work on eradicating this if he wanted the chance of promotion to an Upper Party position.

The vandal tore around the corner into the next street. DV-8 bounded after them. The shadowy figure darted across the road; luckily, DV-8 noticed the pedestrian crossing sign was flashing red. He managed to stop at the edge of the pavement just in time and watched helplessly as the figure reached the other side of the road and the gap between them quickly grew larger. DV-8 glanced anxiously up and down the street; there was no sign of any traffic. Indeed, the roads were closed after curfew, but the pedestrian crossing sign was still red.

He *knew* the rules.

DV-8 locked his eyes on the figure as they swung left into one of the back streets. As soon as the pedestrian crossing sign flashed green, he leapt from the pavement and took off again. He stopped abruptly as the back street was utterly still and silent; there was no sign of the vandal and no way of telling which way they had gone. DV-8 bent forward and clasped his hands to his knees. He wasn't sure if he was just catching his breath from the chase or relieved that he wouldn't have to confront the perpetrator himself.

Once he had caught his breath, he set off to file a *MEURF* (Maintenance Equipment Usage Request Form) so he could clean off the fresh graffiti – a way of fighting against the scourge of deviance he was much more comfortable with.

The events of his nightly patrol were still churning in his mind as he stood in his apartment next to DV-9. The nightly report played out on the infoscreen before them. He could hardly focus on the report, which was a shame as it included a genuinely fascinating piece about pig-iron and the overful-fillment of the Ninth Three-Year Plan. It also meant he didn't notice DV-9 once again staring down at the rip above the right knee of his overalls with great interest. He also failed to note that her breathing rhythm had changed, something he usually liked to keep a close eye on. It was now coming in excited, quick, staccato gasps. The report ended and an exhausted DV-8 heaved his heavy arms across his face and nodded to perform the party salute before turning to retire for the evening.

"Brother?"

DV-8 faced his co-habitant warily, desperate for the end of an already too-eventful day. DV-9 finished saluting, and dropped her arms from in front of her face, revealing a slight rip in her own overalls, just above her left breast. A tiny flicker of smooth, brown skin stood out against the stiff white of her polyester overalls and momentarily caught DV-8's eye through the tear. He quickly averted his gaze upwards and was met by an intense stare from DV-9.

"Yes, sister?"

"I wanted to commend you for taking on additional nightly patrols," she said, her gaze never wavering. "Very diligent of you."

"Thank you…sister."

"Highly commendable."

DV-8 stood perfectly still. His eyes locked onto hers, unable to tear himself away. DV-9 stiffened her posture and inhaled deeply, pushing her chest toward him.

"Um…sister?"

"Yes, brother?"

An ear-splitting silence filled the room; DV-8 was almost too tired to think straight and defaulted to his usual benign politeness.

"You appear to have torn your uniform."

"Oh, dear brother, where?"

He glanced down again, reluctantly, at that shimmering flicker of visible skin.

"There, sister. On your…chest."

"Could you point it out to me, brother?"

"Point it out?" he asked, unsure if the situation was as bizarre as it seemed or if he was delirious from such a tiring day.

"Please, brother," she stared back with well-practised innocence, "as the Supreme Leader always says…"

"We're all in this together."

They completed the motto together. She must have known he would be unable to resist reciting his favourite saying or offering assistance to a fellow party member in the name of the Supreme Leader. He almost felt tricked, but exactly what she was trying to trick him into was unclear.

DV-8 instinctively raised a limp, shaking hand and pointed to the rip in her uniform. DV-9 immediately raised

42

herself up on her toes and pushed her chest towards him, forcing his finger into the tear in the fabric. He stared back at her dumbfounded, unable to process the unprecedented feeling of his finger pressing into warm flesh. She stared deep into his eyes, her rapidly beating heart pulsating through his finger and up his arm as it pressed firmly against her.

"Er...sister?"

"Yes, brother?" she gasped.

"I never told you about my additional patrol, did I?"

"Oh, you can drop the act now! Don't fight it."

DV-8 wrenched his hand away instantly snapping back to reality.

"Sister?" he yelled, raising his voice to the second-highest volume he had ever achieved.

DV-9 pushed her whole body up against his and wrapped her arms around his neck. DV-8 wriggled free and began backing away in astonishment.

"It's OK!" she protested. "I always knew you were one of us. The rip in your uniform, genius! An act of deviance in broad daylight, right under their stupid noses!"

He glanced down and horrified, spotted the rip just above the right knee of his overalls.

"Just small enough you could claim it was an accident," she continued, stalking him across the apartment as he backed away towards the far wall.

DV-8 startled as he bumped up against the wall-mounted infoscreen and realised there was nowhere left to run. DV-9 thrust herself against him once again and stared longingly into his eyes.

"I used to think you were just like the rest of them. But you are so much more!" She moaned and pressed her lips against his.

Something ignited inside DV-8. He grabbed her by the shoulders, spun her around and pushed her up against the infoscreen. He leaned into her, and DV-9 closed her eyes, awaiting the embrace she had desperately longed for but dared never to dream of. DV-8 reached past her and pressed the glowing red button beside the screen.

- IV -

ON THE TRAIN TO WORK, DV-8 found himself troubled by the events of the previous evening. Although he had always hoped for an opportunity to save a fellow party member from the clutches of deviance, he struggled to focus on the day's work ahead. He was surprised at the absence of pride and satisfaction that his actions merited and puzzled by the strange emptiness and vague anxiety pervading his thoughts.

He listened to the commuter train's low hum and replayed the previous evening's events over in his mind, searching for the source of his discomfort. He was sure that he had done the right thing. He could even picture how proud his Sensitivity Trainer would be of him; he had followed the manual that she provided to the letter. After all, his cohabitant's behaviour showed clear signs of deviance that had to be addressed immediately. He was sure DV-9 would have said the same herself had she been in a clearer state of mind and had the security officers' intervention not rendered her unconscious. The level of force employed by the security officers when they came to collect her had slightly perturbed him, but he had never worked in the re-education department and assumed they knew best. There was one thing he was now much less confused about; the security officers had made the purpose of the iron heel that all Party issued boots were fitted with abundantly clear.

He suspected his unease with the whole affair may come from a sense of guilt. After all, the tear in his overalls had clearly sparked something in DV-9. Had he spotted the infraction earlier, he obviously would have addressed it immediately, especially if he had known what was to come.

One thing he could feel relieved about, was that even if he couldn't be sure of DV-9's exact fate, he could be confident that she wouldn't be subjected to a long, drawn-out trial. The legal reforms had been one of the Supreme Leader's most benevolent acts during his reign. Party members no longer had to suffer the indignity of a public trial or incur the high costs of legal representation. Trials had been scrapped altogether, and all legal proceedings were carried out and decided by a small, unknown group of magistrates in secret.

When reporting DV-9, he had offered to supply the security officers with a testimonial to use as evidence, but they informed him this would not be necessary. He couldn't help but be impressed by the ease and efficiency with which the magistrates carried out such matters, lifting the burden of having to defend oneself off the back of the accused during what must already be an incredibly stressful time. As this was surely her first offence, DV-8 theorised, her sentence would probably not be too harsh. Until last night, she had been an up-standing Party member, as far as he knew. DV-8 mentioned this to the security officers as he dropped off the few belongings he found under DV-9's bed; a box of a dozen or so yellow spray paint cans and a black balaclava. He wasn't sure what she had used these for. Perhaps she had been volunteering for the art department and was working on the latest mural depicting the first and only recorded lunar and solar eclipse which reportedly occurred simultaneously at the moment of the Supreme Leader's birth. Whatever they were for, DV-8 asked that they be returned to DV-9 as soon as she was feeling better. The security officers assured him they would and took the box from him with much interest.

The train stopped abruptly and jolted him out of his memories. He looked up to see the slight, brittle woman who had caught his eye during the weekly report sitting across from him, staring down intently. He followed her gaze and was horrified to see that the offending rip in his trousers was still there. In all the excitement, he had forgotten to repair it before leaving for work that mourning. He clasped his hand over his knee, covering up the hint of flesh underneath, lest it unleash similarly animalistic, desirous urges in her too. Shame and embarrassment coursed through him.

The brittle woman eyed him suspiciously and reached inside her top pocket for her e-notebook. As she disembarked from the train, he couldn't help but notice that her breathing rate had increased, similar to how DV-9 had reacted the night before. He only hoped she could control herself and that it wasn't too late for her to resist his undeniable yet unintended charms.

DV-8 resolved to repair the rip as soon as possible and to always remain conscious of the seemingly irresistible effect he had on female party members from now on.

Arriving at work, he was thankful to find an exciting assignment waiting for him that might help him take his mind off the previous evening's events. Once he had sewn the rip in the leg of his overalls, his attention turned to the week's written account of the Supreme Leader's overseas tour he had received from the Senior Leadership team.

The written account reported that the Supreme Leader had given a speech at the UN on 'deviance suppression'. The speech was well received by the other world leaders in attendance, but unfortunately, it had not been filmed or recorded: his task was to produce the video evidence. Although every single action and utterance was outlined clearly in the written account, some details were unaccounted for and generously left for his imagination to fill in the blanks. For example, the exact shade of red of the Supreme Leader's tie was not specified and would need to be embellished. DV-8 relished any assignment that allowed him to flex his creative muscles and set about creating the footage for inclusion in the upcoming weekly report.

"Excuse me, brother," said a familiar voice.

DV-8 looked up to see BB-01 beaming down at him once again. BB-01 crossed his arms across his face and delivered the party salute. DV-8 reciprocated in kind.

"Just wanted to thank you for attending to my patrol last night."

"You're welcome, brother. We're all in this together, after all," DV-8 answered, trying to continue with his work.

"Of course," BB-01 sniggered involuntarily, "I trust the patrol was uneventful?"

At that moment, a surprising resistance overcame DV-8. Thankfully not 'The Resistance' but a resistance to share the events of the nightly patrol with BB-01. Perhaps it was the annoyance at being distracted from such a captivating assignment, or maybe he was still tired from the night before, but what DV-8 said next was completely unprecedented.

"Indeed, brother."

It was an odd feeling, and not one he had ever experienced, to proffer an expression which was not entirely reflective of the events in question. Especially to a superior.

"Glad to hear it. I like to keep a pretty tight ship in my quarter."

DV-8 still wasn't sure where the cause for his deception had come from. Most likely it was the memory of BB-01 yawning during the weekly report. Although DV-8 was inclined to give people the benefit of the doubt, he wasn't stupid. From that moment on, he knew he needed to play his cards close to his chest when dealing with him. DV-8 began tapping away at his computer again, keen to get back to the task at hand and failing to notice the curious smile that BB-01 now regarded him with.

"I trust you also realise," BB-01 continued, to the further annoyance of DV-8, "that I wouldn't have missed a patrol unless my other engagement was of the utmost importance."

"Of course, brother."

BB-01 leant down, bringing his face inches away from that of his increasingly beleaguered comrade.

"I was actually attending a highly productive senior leadership meeting regarding the latest deviance suppression initiative." BB-01 lowered his voice so as not to be overheard, and DV-8 lowered his chair so as not to be in such close proximity to his colleague. "Between you and me, the end may be just around the corner."

"I certainly hope so, brother."

DV-8 eyed BB-01 suspiciously as he marched away down the corridor.

He spent the rest of the day creating and perfecting the visual evidence of the Supreme Leader's speech at the UN summit. DV-8 uploaded the lines of dialogue provided in the written account and played the footage back. He reclined and admired his handiwork; the elusive sense of pride that failed to accompany his actions of the previous evening rose up within him as he watched the completed report play out. He settled on antique ruby red for the tie in the end, an old favourite. He frowned as the speech ended with the Supreme Leaders' final line:

My friends, the end may be just around the corner.

A massive cheer from the watching audience, which he had been specifically instructed to include, rang out and he turned the words over in his mind. Before he had time to turn them too far, he was distracted by a deafening fanfare which blasted out across the office.

This signalled the end of the workday and the beginning of the worknight.

DV-8 sprang to his feet, performed the party salute in unison with his colleagues and filed out of the office, forgetting what it was he'd been turning over in his mind as he made his way to the weekly meeting.

The weekly meetings had been introduced so that party members could come together regularly, in an attempt to engender a sense of camaraderie and community. All residents of a particular ward were encouraged to attend, especially by the encouragement wardens and their encouragement dogs. The meetings were a chance to raise any issues for discussion, report any incidents they had encountered during the nightly patrols and formally accuse any of their fellow party members they felt were exhibiting signs of deviance.

DV-8 sat near the front row of the large gathering inside his local meeting hall, staring at the three members of the

Senior Leadership team who presided over the meeting. They sat at a long table in front of the infoscreen on the front wall, looking out at the blank faces of the party members, patiently waiting for the meeting to begin. They remained in complete silence for three minutes until the clock above the infoscreen ticked over to eighteen minutes past the hour. The senior leadership team immediately sprang to their feet, crossed their arms across their faces and nodded, performing the party salute. DV-8 leapt to his feet along with the rest of the crowd and reciprocated in kind.

"WEEKLY MEETING, ward one-one-eight commencing," trumpeted a stern-looking woman with taut features sitting in the centre of the three Senior Leaders. Her serial number was 1N-XS.

DV-8 sat back down, glanced around and saw BB-01 arriving late, hurriedly searching for his seat near the back of the room.

"ITEM ONE – deviance. Incidents and accusations. Please begin," 1N-XS announced.

She had been an excellent Senior Leader for the ward, DV-8 thought, rising through the ranks thanks to her fanatical devotion to the Supreme Leader, tireless vigilance and strict adherence to the law of The Party. Though she had settled down into her management role somewhat in recent years, outside of the weekly meetings she rarely contributed to any special projects or spear-headed any new initiatives. These days, she was an adequate district representative and carried out the traditional role of Senior Leader with quiet conscientiousness. In other words, he was a big fan of 1N-XS's early work but felt they had become a bit mainstream over time.

The weekly procedure began; each party member stood-up in turn, reported any incidents they had recorded from their nightly patrols that had not been dealt with, made any accusations they felt necessary, and returned to their seats. The party member next to them would repeat the exercise, and so on. As the front row of members delivered their weekly updates, DV-8 looked down at his notebook and the entry he had made during the weekly report concerning BB-01. He knew that by all reasonable standards, he had cause to make a formal accusation. Still, for some reason, he was hesitant, anxious even as the updates continued and his turn to deliver his report to the Senior Leaders grew closer and closer.

He glanced back again to try to spot BB-01, but his eye was caught by two security officers standing at the back of the room in their black uniforms. He found it odd that his recent opportunities to report and rescue UB-40 and DV-9 from the clutches of deviance did not embolden his resolve to save other such wayward comrades. Curiously, the memories of their arrests actually made him more reluctant to report BB-01 now that he had the chance. Perhaps the nature of his former roommate's transfer for re-education and the security officers' somewhat robust tactics gave him pause for thought. DV-8 abhorred violence and unrest of any kind. The fact that deviant party members' actions often made violence towards themselves a necessity was deplorable and must cause much discomfort to the security officers who are forced to dole it out. He always tried to remember that these were unwell people not acting in their right minds.

DV-8 tapped the stylus against the notebook nervously and continued to stare at the serial number written in it, 'BB-01'.

"NEXT! D-V Eight!" 1N-XS's barked instruction forced DV-8 to his feet.

"Serial number D-V Eight," he began, still unsure of his intentions, "All nightly patrols conducted successfully. Two acts of resistance vandalism were recorded and removed on blocks nine and seventeen."

He went to speak again but faltered. In the blank infoscreen he saw the shadowy reflection of the two security officers watching closely from the back of the room. The Senior Leaders looked up from scribbling their notes with raised eyebrows at his hesitation.

"No accusations to make at this time." DV-8 returned to his seat and exhaled deeply before quickly collecting himself.

"Very good. NEXT!"

The meeting continued as usual, with the rest of the party members giving their updates. Eventually, it was BB-01's turn, and he sprang to his feet with enthusiasm.

"Serial number B-B zero one. All nightly patrols conducted without incident. No accusations to make at this time."

DV-8 allowed himself another glance back and noted BB-01's rigid posture and diligent expression. Once again, he was privately pleased that he had given someone the benefit of the doubt, even if it was something he wouldn't be keen to share with anybody else.

"Very good. NEXT!" 1N-XS barked once again. Any lower Party member would of course be written up for excessive barking at this point, but the Senior Leaders needed certain dispensations to carry out their roles effectively.

DV-8 returned to facing forward with a slight, contented smile and resolved to enjoy the rest of the weekly meeting as usual.

"Forgive me, party leader," BB-01 called from the back of the room as he stood up again, "D-V Eight."

DV-8 was not scared by the prospect of re-education as some of his fellow Party members seemed to be. In fact, on several occasions, he had considered volunteering for a stay in a re-education camp. This would ensure he was at minimal risk of succumbing to deviance and that his resolve and commitment to the Supreme Leader were as strong as possible. However, when he heard his own serial number called out in the context of an accusation, he felt his heart stop for some reason. He couldn't fully process what was happening, and his breath evacuated his lungs at an alarming rate.

1N-XS craned her neck to see BB-01 standing at the back of the room, "Accusation, brother?" she asked with an intrigue bordering on excitement.

DV-8 was in shock. Never had he even suspected he may be accused of deviance at a weekly meeting. Perhaps it was warranted though, he thought. After all, one could succumb to deviance and not even know it. As Senior Leaders often warned:

Deviants did not always know they were Deviants.

When DV-8 first heard this, he became terrified that he might be a deviant without realising it. Over time he became so concerned and anxious that he sought advice from one of the state-sponsored therapists. He shared his fear that he was a secret deviant and didn't know it. He was quickly reassured. The therapist reminded him that, yes, while deviants can be deviants without knowing it, deviants can also be incredibly deceptive, strangely seductive, and even charming. After meeting with DV-8, she said he had absolutely no worries on that front whatsoever.

He couldn't bring himself to turn around and face his accuser, focusing instead on maintaining his ubiquitous, benign smile, which usually required no effort and normally came to him quite naturally.

"No, forgive me again, Party leader," BB-01 replied, "I'm afraid I neglected to mention that I did not complete all my nightly patrols. One of them was carried out by D-V Eight in my absence."

Though his expression never faltered, DV-8 couldn't help deflating slightly into his chair as a wave of relief washed over him.

"I just wanted to express my gratitude and recommend a commendation," BB-01 continued from the back of the room, "I'm sure with party members like him, the end of the war on deviance may be just around the corner."

DV-8 finally let go of the breath he had been holding ever since BB-01 called out his serial number but promptly gulped it back in as he started up again, "Although, D-V Eight did fail to mention the act of vandalism he encountered on my patrol route?"

He tensed up again as the Senior Leader barked from the front of the room, "D-V EIGHT?"

"Apologies, Party leader," he managed to splutter as he slowly rose to his feet, "It seems I forgot I encountered the infraction on the additional route, not my own."

He turned slowly to face BB-01, "Thank you for the correction, brother."

"Not at all, brother," BB-01 smiled broadly back at him, "we're all in this together, after all."

"Well, try to be more careful next time," 1N-XS waved dismissively in their direction. "ITEM NUMBER TWO..."

DV-8 slumped back down in his chair. The weekly meeting carried on, but he barely registered anything else that was said. He couldn't stop thinking about BB-01 and how he felt more wary of him than ever.

After the meeting, on his journey home and during the nightly message from the Supreme Leader, he couldn't stop thinking about BB-01 and the events of the weekly meeting. Although he was grateful to have his error pointed out and admired the diligence BB-01 had shown, something in his smile told DV-8 that his superior was still not to be trusted.

He couldn't quite put his finger on why.

DV-8 stood in the centre of the room alone and watched the nightly report play out on the infoscreen. A different, new but still fairly old white-haired man sat at the desk, almost identical to his colleague who delivered the previous night's nightly report. The same much younger, blonder woman sat next to him as he addressed the viewers.

"Party members are being advised to be extra vigilant during their commutes tomorrow as a missile strike from our enemies across the pond has been reported as imminent."

DV-8 listened but barely registered what was being said.

"Of course, The Resistance are trying to use this to their advantage as usual, spreading a vicious rumour that these are our own missiles which were launched yesterday and have malfunctioned, turning back on their trajectory and are now primed to strike in the heart of our own capital. The fact is, no missile launch took place yesterday from the south-coast military base and anyone claiming that it did should be reported as an agent of The Resistance at your earliest convenience. They really will say anything to push their deviant agenda, huh?"

"Actually…" the young woman began.

A loud fanfare bleated out from the infoscreen.

"And that is your nightly report," the white-haired man interrupted, "goodnight, everybody and remember, stay vigilant."

So distracted was he that as DV-8 retired for the night, he couldn't even bring himself to read *The Book* as he usually did. He lay in bed, struggling to sleep. Only when he noticed something curious could he drive BB-01 and the weekly meeting from his mind.

After lights out, no one was permitted to leave their quarters, not even to enter the main, shared rooms of the apartments. The heating and lighting were shut off to discourage unnecessary fraternisation between co-habitants. All party member's quarters were reinforced with soundproof cladding to ensure sleep was not disturbed by any necessary interventions of the security officers elsewhere in the building or by the incessant chiming of the clocks since the change to new time.

Although he was lying in total darkness and complete silence as usual, DV-8 thought he could somehow sense the absence of his old cohabitant DV-9. It was as if something was different since she left, even though everything appeared just the same. He finally fell asleep to the thought that this was the first night he had spent entirely alone in his whole life.

- V -

THE BOOK HAD NOT ALWAYS been the only book authorised for publication and read widely by Party members. There had been other select titles distributed throughout the population with the blessing of the Supreme Leader over the years. That was, until the great literary purge came into effect. It was an average day like any other when the order suddenly came that all other books were to be destroyed and that reading any other books was now prohibited. To ensure their message was fully understood, The Party organised mass book burnings where they set fire to any other publications they could find amongst the populace. The purge was swift, decisive, and effective. The only mishap came when a team of book burners were tasked with destroying all available copies of an ancient book called *War and Peace*; the blaze quickly got out of control and burned down several local government buildings, including the fire station.

The popularity and proliferation of audiobooks and e-books also meant that eradicating all other publications proved more complicated than first thought. The audio files and digital copies of these books could easily be deleted, but this wouldn't have quite the theatrical and symbolic effect The Party was hoping for. They were forced to hold a second mass book burning during which all other available audio-books or e-books were 'burned' in the more modern sense of the word – the digital files were copied onto compact discs or 'CDs'. Then a third mass book burning where the CDs were burned again, this time in the more traditional sense – on a big fire.

In a rush to enact the great literary purge, the Supreme Leader's entire private library, which was to be the only collection of books spared from the flames, had been destroyed by mistake. For months afterwards, teams of writers had to work around the clock recreating many of the literary masterpieces from memory before the Supreme Leader could realise what had happened. He enjoyed many of these titles even to this day, including his favourites: *The Merchant of Venus, The Killer Mockingbird, The Good Gatsby* and *Animal Farm*. Although he remembered Animal Farm being a little more adult and bleaker, he still enjoyed the quaint children's tale of pigs, horses and all the other animals banding together to save the farm and learn the importance of friendship, nonetheless. The Senior Leaders were keen to re-produce a particular book as it was one of the Supreme Leader's favourites. They could remember the name of the author, Joseph Heller, and the basics of the story which revolved around a cowardly fighter pilot in the U.S. Air Force. However, the title had long been forgotten and try as they might, they just couldn't remember it. The only person likely to remember the title was the Supreme Leader himself but they couldn't ask him as this would reveal their mistake in having burned his private library to the ground in the first place. It was a real catch-22 situation.

One of the more popular titles before the great purge was *It Can't Happen Here*. It was an ancient book by a foreign author whose name and native land had since been lost in the annals of time but, for a long time, was a favourite among Party members. The story was a lament that the Supreme Leader's authority and the ideology of The Party had not taken root in the author's homeland and that it likely never would. It was an attack on the society and other people around the author whose loose morals and deviant tendencies meant that the Supreme Leader would likely never deem them worthy of his leadership or inclusion in The Party. 'It can't happen here, why oh why can't it happen here?' was the author's final cry at the conclusion of the story.

Though he was only a child then, DV-8 vividly remembered the day the great purge came into effect. He had been reading one of the few story books still authorised for publication, *Moby Dick*. It was a very popular read, and once the purge began, it could be found wherever books were burned. He was only a few chapters in but was enjoying the story, despite the national anthem blaring from the infoscreen at the foot of his bed. The door burst open, and a jackbooted security officer came barrelling in. The officer ripped the book from his hands, examined the front cover and spat down on the ground in disgust.

DV-8 tried to protest in his earnest, childish way: "You know you're not supposed to judge a book by its..."

"Silence!" the security officer bellowed. "This is unauthorised, propagandic filth!"

With that, the officer set the book alight. DV-8 could still remember seeing the flames crawl across the pages, devouring them and the black ash floating slowly to the floor in the security officer's wake as he stormed out in search of more contraband.

Today, DV-8 recognised The Party's great service in enacting the purge and was grateful for their protection from potentially deviant ideas and corrupting writing. However, he had been enjoying *Moby Dick* and, as a much younger, more precocious man, had sought an illegal copy. On occasion, he would sneak off and visit one of the few remaining small antique stores that could still be found in the Plebeian quarters in the hope of coming across a copy. Alas, he never could find one, try as he might. The book came to represent something forever unattainable for him, an impossible goal that would never be realised. He often thought about the book and remarked, "It's like my own personal white whale...whatever that means."

His second favourite book survived the first purge as it was authored by the Supreme Leader himself, but even this was eventually outlawed. It was a small book of the Supreme

Leader's most famous and inspiring quotations, containing such gems as:

'The only thing we have to fear is fear itself.'
'Ask not what your country can do for you; ask what you can do for your country.'

And DV-8's personal favourite:

'If you want the rainbow, you've got to put up with the rain.'

There was a myriad of quotes on a vast array of political, cultural, and philosophical topics, displaying the Supreme Leader's endless wit and insightful, contemplative nature. Indeed, it was hard to believe that one man had coined so many unforgettable sayings. In truth, they weren't all entirely his own work; some were improvements on well-known phrases made famous by others. The Supreme Leader agreed with the sentiment of William Shakespeare's famous quote, 'Brevity is the soul of wit', but he found it a little wordy. Thanks to the Supreme Leader's superior intellect, the quote had been subtly altered and was included in the book as the more concise and much improved 'Brevity: the soul of wit'.

His corrections to other popular expressions proved so incisive it almost rendered them obsolete. Take, for example, 'Clothes make the man'. The Supreme Leader rightly pointed out that, in truth, it is in fact quite the reverse. He also expanded on other famous sayings, resulting in far more insightful observations such as the much-improved adage, 'It's a dog-eat-dog world…and vice versa'. However, there was one quote in the book that DV-8 struggled to understand:

'The definition of insanity is doing the same thing over and over again and expecting a different result.'

He became fixated on this quotation as it was the only one in the book that did not resonate with him. He would read the line repeatedly, over and over again, each time expecting the Supreme Leader's superior knowledge to shine through and to be struck with inspiration, but to no avail. Far be it from him to question the wisdom of the Supreme Leader, he thought, but he couldn't understand why it was so wrong to expect a better outcome each time you attempted something. Was it wrong to be optimistic? If you genuinely believe you are doing the right thing, why would you deviate from your chosen course of action? If you changed what you were doing based purely on the outcomes, wouldn't that suggest you didn't honestly believe in what you were doing in the first place?

These questions would trouble DV-8 each time he tried to understand the meaning of the quotation and why he was relieved when these kinds of books became prohibited too. It meant he would no longer have to grapple with such complex questions.

He always carried out his party duties in the same way, with enthusiasm and diligence, following the same strict schedule he had followed for as long as he could remember. Although the war on deviance had not yet been completely won, he believed wholeheartedly in the cause and his methods. He greeted every mourning with a renewed hope that today would be the day the war was finally won. In other words, he attempted the same thing over and over again, always expecting a different result. If that was the definition of insanity, he thought, then you could go ahead and call him insane. He secretly believed that this rare oversight on the part of the Supreme Leader may have been why The Party came to ban all such books.

Unfortunately for such a creature of habit as DV-8, it had been a week of firsts; he had always fostered a strong dislike for firsts:

- Firstly, and therefore most egregiously, he had seen his first evidence of the rumoured 'Resistance' in the form of graffiti daubed on an infoscreen.
- He had been called upon during the weekly meeting for the first time.
- He had spent his first night alone, without a co-habitant.
- He had cause to report a fellow party member for deviance in the form of UB-40, the secret book owner, for the first time.

It had also been a week of seconds:

o   He had seen his second piece of evidence of the ru-
     moured 'Resistance' in the form of the secret book.
o   He had cause to report a fellow party member for de-
     viance in the form of DV-9, his former roommate,
     for the second time.

Unfortunately, his dislike of seconds was second only to his
dislike of firsts. His favourite things to do were to carry out
nightly patrols, contribute to the weekly reports and attend
the weekly meetings. He had now completed these 7,300
times, 1042 times and 956 times, respectively, and was
pleased that each time he carried out one of these tasks, he
moved further and further away from any form of firsts.

   The clock struck forty-two minutes past the hour and a
fanfare blared out and awoke DV-8. The blinds opened automatically, and he sat bolt upright, ready to take on the day
just as he did every other day. This familiar mourning routine immediately brought him some comfort, and he resolved to take on the day with his characteristic, some might
say, pathological optimism. He sprang out of bed, hoping
that he had seen the last of any firsts for a good while.

   He found a renewed appreciation for his routine over the
next few days: he went to work, conducted his nightly patrols, and attended the quarterly lecture series, *Free Speech*.
So called as these were speeches which any Party member

was welcome to attend, free of charge. This particular talk was on the virtues of censorship.

The next night he attended one of the regular showings of *The Film*. He took a moment to appreciate the calm that a few uneventful days had brought him and looked back around the theatre. The familiar sight of the flat, silent faces of his fellow party members, eyes glazed, mouths agape, staring at the screen transfixed, warmed his heart. He saw the slight, brittle woman he had seen on the train a few days ago. She sat a couple of rows ahead of him. He allowed his gaze to linger on her for a moment as the character of Winston spoke on screen, his words echoing around the auditorium, "I love you."

"Pervert!" The slight woman spat at the screen, exhibiting a force and venom that contrasted sharply with her petite frame. She even managed to startle some of the party members sitting around her, rousing them from their stupors into joining her condemnation of the film's main villain. DV-8 settled back in his chair with a contented smile to watch *The Film* for the 5,343rd time.

Following the screening he returned home and watched the nightly report as he always did but with a fresh appreciation and attentiveness. A third news reporter, perhaps the oldest and most white-haired yet, sat at the desk and delivered that evening's report.

"The missiles landed in the north-east quadrant of the city but thankfully, as evidenced by eye-witness reports, the effect was minimal," he reported confidently. "A bus stop was damaged almost to the point of being unusable. This just goes to show that our enemies are not as well equipped as they would like us to…"

He trailed off and looked off screen, distracted as his ever-present, young blonde co-host smiled out at the viewers.

"Excuse me for a moment."

The man disappeared off camera, after a brief pause and some concerned glances from his co-host, a different man returned to the desk and continued the report.

"These events were of course all part of a planned exercise designed to show off the Supreme Leader's expertise in bomb diffusion and a demonstration of our defence capabilities and latest technological innovations," the replacement anchor continued. "This is a clear message to our enemies that any attack on party soil would be absolutely futile. The exercise began with a take-off from the south-coast military base a few days ago. We know some nasty rumours circulated about this event, some even claiming this was a genuine attack from our enemies; but we can assure you, this was always a planned demonstration, and it was an unmitigated success. Anyone who claimed this did not take place as reported has been dealt with and anyone you hear repeating these scurrilous rumours should be considered a member of The Resistance and dealt with accordingly."

He looked to his young but more experienced co-host as an awkward silence filled the screen.

"Anything you'd like to add?"

"No, thank you," she replied politely, making sure her beaming smile stayed presented to the audience at all times.

"Well, that's about all we've got time for..."

DV-8 retired for the evening, the renewal of his usual routines settling his mind and allowing for an excellent night's sleep.

DV-8 craved routine so much, that he found himself slipping into a new one over the next few days without realising. Every day, around the same time, he would look up from his work console expecting to see BB-01's aggressively avuncular smile leering down at him as it had done the previous few days. Although DV-8 enjoyed additional tasks and overtime, for some reason, he dreaded another request or inquiry coming from BB-01. It was a relief each time he looked up and didn't see the face peering around his cubicle wall.

He was pleased to be able to focus solely on his work, creating the visual evidence of the Supreme Leader's latest overseas rally. As he put the finishing touches to the footage, he stared into the benevolent, warm eyes of the Supreme Leader, which he himself had created on the work console just a few minutes earlier. Everything was going to be OK, he thought to himself. He remembered the secret book owner, UB-40 and his former roommate, DV-9 and daydreamed about how they would soon be cured and back to living productive, happy non-deviant lives. Even his concerns about BB-01 seemed to melt away; with such a leader in charge, DV-8 was as confident as ever that the end to the war on deviance was just around the corner.

We're all in this together, he said to himself in a moment of inspiration, then switched off his work console and prepared for the end of the workday.

He packed away his things, straightened his desk and sat patiently awaiting the daily fanfare which signalled all party members could leave work for the evening. The clocks struck twenty-three minutes past the hour.

Quitting time.

But no fanfare came.

In its place, an eerie, all-consuming silence spread like a mist through the office. DV-8's eyes flitted between the clock and the infoscreen. For as long as he could remember, the screen had emitted the fanfare at precisely this time every day without fail.

Never a second late or a second early.

The silence continued, spreading uncertainty and apprehension through the party members who remained sat at their desks, waiting. The longer the disparity between the time that the fanfare should have sounded and it actually sounding, the more concerned DV-8 grew. As the seconds slowly ticked by, the dread grew inside him until, mercifully, the silence was broken, not by the fanfare however, but by something entirely different – a deafening explosion.

DV-8 gripped his workstation in an attempt to steady himself. The ringing in his ears was starting to dissipate from the noise of the first blast when another rocked the entire office building once again. The panic and fear that possessed him was like nothing he had ever felt before. He stayed rooted to the spot and scanned his surroundings instinctively, trying to process what was happening. What could have made such a sound and caused an entire office block to shake the way it had?

His eyes darted around the room, and he soon saw an even more alarming sight. Some of his colleagues had left their workstations before hearing the fanfare signalling the end of the working day. He felt the same panic as them, the same terror at what had just occurred, but he also knew that standards had to be kept, even in exceptional circumstances.

Several of his colleagues cautiously crept over to the enormous window which ran the length of the far wall, facing out across the rest of the city toward the party HQ. Reaching for the notebook in his top pocket, DV-8 began scribbling down the serial numbers of his less diligent colleagues who were now congregating by the window. An excited murmuring spread amongst them.

DV-8 flinched as a great, mechanical roaring noise cut through the air, different to the first two sounds which had reverberated up through the foundations of the building.

This noise passed over their heads and screeched away across the city.

He quickly collected himself and resumed his reporting. But as more and more Party members joined the crowd forming at the window, he found it increasingly difficult to keep up and successfully record everyone's serial number.

Another sound then filled the office, one which troubled DV-8 even more than the ones that came before. It was the sound of his colleagues crying out in unison, but not with the harmony that such a gathering would usually have when reciting a Party anthem or hymn, which he always enjoyed very much. No, this was a collective din made up of all sorts of tones, pitches and volumes, a guttural howl, an expression of something, but what it was exactly, he had no idea.

He looked on in astonishment as one of the gathered crowd dropped to their knees and raised their clenched fists high in the air, as if their deviance was causing some kind of involuntary convulsion. Others began embracing each other, and all the while, the barbaric roar of the crowd echoed around the usually silent office. DV-8 watched in astonishment as the group began stampeding out of the office as one, not with the order and grace of a military procession but with a fevered, pack mentality that frightened him further still.

"They did it! They really did it!" He heard one of them shriek as the herd thundered past his cubicle.

They did what? DV-8 thought to himself. What had the crowd seen through the window to cause such a display of unrestrained joy and deviance? He remembered The Party had been working on a new design for the party flag for some years now; rumour had it that they would go with a slightly lighter shade of white. Had the new flags been unveiled and displayed across the city, is that what they were celebrating? Although he could certainly understand their excitement if that was the case, it was no excuse for the type of behaviour they were now exhibiting. He had heard of cases of mass deviance before, but only in overseas reports. He never thought he would see such an outbreak so close to home, in his office, of all places. The animalistic wailing died out as the crowd fled the office.

DV-8 stayed glued to his chair alongside a handful of his other, more assiduous colleagues. He stayed at his workstation for hours, eagerly awaiting the familiar fanfare that heralded an update from The Party. He did his best to ignore the concerning, far-off deep thuds and rumblings that continued long after everyone had bolted. It was only when the scheduled time of his nightly patrol drew near that he knew he had to act. He had never missed a nightly patrol and was damned if he was going to start now. He elected to leave and attend to his Party duty as usual, certain there would be some update in the Supreme Leader's broadcast later that night to help explain the unexpected and unprecedented events of the day.

The train home was unusually empty. By DV-8's best estimate, it seemed there was about a third of the number of commuters travelling back to their quarters as usual, an assessment which also happened to be precisely accurate. He assumed that many of the missing Party members had been called upon to help with whatever situation was unfolding across the city. He felt calmed by this thought and reassured that the situation would soon be under control, and they would be advised on what was happening in the nightly report. The mood on the train was odd, the complete silence they maintained had never felt uncomfortable before, but today it did, as if there was something that should be said, needed to be said, that was being ignored.

The silence became almost unbearable as the train rumbled through the Senior Leadership district, and dark, black smoke from several buildings floated in through their carriage window. They tried their best to stifle their coughs and shield their eyes from the smoke with as little fuss as possible, and still, no one said a word for the rest of the journey. DV-8 knew something needed to be done as the silence became intolerable. Someone had to step up and take action, to address the elephant in the room and break the tension that now filled every available space not already occupied by thick, black smoke. Almost instinctively, he took action. He stood up, stepped forward and closed the window before returning to his seat and carrying on his journey in renewed silence.

During the 7,300 nightly patrols he had carried out, DV-8 had reported just three instances of deviant activity; the two times he had encountered the graffiti in the last week or so and once several years ago when he noticed a portrait of the Supreme Leader hanging at a particularly unseemly angle through an apartment window.

However, that night on his patrol, he reported over one hundred instances of deviant activity; graffiti, property damage, arson and several more examples of portraits of the Supreme Leader hung at even more unseemly angles. Some angles were so unseemly that the portraits were not hanging at all but lying damaged and discarded in the middle of the street! He meticulously scribbled each offence down in his electronic notebook and only stopped when the memory card reached capacity, and he was unable to record any more of his findings.

He found such a stark increase in deviant behaviour alarming, but what was even more perplexing was the ominous, rhythmic thumping sound that continued throughout the night coming from the direction of the party headquarters. He thought he heard a large crowd cheering on a few occasions, but his route was too far from the party HQ to investigate further, and he was sure there would be some update to explain the day's strange events in the evening broadcast.

To his surprise, when he returned to his quarters for the evening, not only was there no update, but there was also no broadcast at all! He stood in the centre of the room facing the cold, blank stare of the infoscreen for almost two hours, but no such message ever materialised. He steeled himself to do the unthinkable, break protocol and retire for the evening before the evening report was broadcast. After another hour spent building up enough courage, he was about to step away when the familiar fanfare rang out, rooting him to the spot and sending a spark of relief running up his spine. The relief quickly mutated into a tingling of anxiety that spread across his whole body as a familiar face filled the screen but not the one he had expected or hoped to see.

"Brothers! Sisters!" It was the smiling, relentlessly avuncular face of BB-01. "We've taken control of the party HQ. It's time for the resistance to begin. The war on deviance is over!"

DV-8 stood still, trying to make sense of what he saw but failing miserably. The shaking camera, the face that didn't belong on the infoscreen, and the use of contractions like 'we've' instead of proper, formal English. The whole scene felt impossible and made him and his surroundings feel almost unreal.

BB-01 stepped back to reveal he was surrounded by a small group of soldiers all dressed in black.

"If you're ready to join the fight, we are amassing at Party HQ. So come and join us! Come join the party! After all, we're all in this together!" BB-01 raised a fist high into the air and cheered; the soldiers around him reciprocated in kind.

The infoscreen cut to black, and the silence emitting from it filled the room like a poisonous gas. DV remained where he was, but he now felt he was at the centre of a huge void, a vast empty space. The walls, the ceiling, even the floor felt like they expanded out, off into the distance surrounding him, leaving nothing to hold him up or keep him from coming apart himself. The uncanny feeling that this impossible sight engendered in him was intolerable. He began to shake as if his body was compelling him to do something, anything in response to what he had just witnessed. He knew he had to act, and so he did. Almost by instinct, he took the electronic notebook from his top pocket. He swiped to the entry he had previously made regarding BB-01 and put a tick in the CONFIRMED column, satisfied he now had enough evidence to confirm that BB-01 was not entirely what he seemed to be. The red line struck through the serial number, and the familiar, light-hearted jingle accompanied the animated thumbs up on the screen. It was nowhere near as satisfying to him as it once would have been.

That night, DV-8 lay in bed anxiously awaiting another fanfare – the real fanfare – signalling the admittedly late but no less welcome, start of a message from the Senior Leaders offering some sort of explanation or guidance. It never came. Eventually, he succumbed to exhaustion and fell asleep.

The next mourning, the clocks struck forty-two minutes past the hour. No fanfare sounded and the blinds did not open automatically but DV-8 sat bolt upright in his bed, regardless. Right on time, just as he'd done every mourning for as long as he could remember. Desperate as he was to stick to the same routine as always, despite the creeping feeling that nothing would ever be the same again.

- VI -

FOR THE PAST DECADE, The Party slogan had been 'Can't Complain', but with the proviso that the word 'Can't' must always be underlined whenever the slogan was written or heavily emphasised whenever it was spoken. The Party had been working to shorten the slogan over the years. This current version was a big improvement on the previous slogan of, *nolite solliciti esse felix vel aliud*, which was Latin for 'Don't worry, be happy, or else'. That mourning however, it was one of the much older slogans that came to DV-8's mind; although it had only been in use long before he was born and he had only seen it in history textbooks, it did provide some comfort in such troubling times – *Keep Calm and Carry On*.

It was precisely what he intended to do, and he recited the words in his mind as he boarded the train for work just as he did every other day.

Unfortunately, even repeating the soothing words couldn't distract him from the fact that the train was even more empty than he had found it on his journey home the previous evening. The carriage was unoccupied save for himself, the brittle woman he had seen at the theatre just a few days ago and, sat next to her, a rotund rosy-cheeked male party member. DV-8 could not recall having seen the man before but, from the look of him, he suspected this party member had been claiming more than his allotted share of food rations or neglecting his mandatory daily calisthenic exercises. The contents of the weekly food parcels changed regularly, and the man was clearly a big fan of the most recent offering. For the past few months, they had consisted mainly of Soylent Greens, a polarising choice; some loved it while others weren't so keen. This was understandable as the taste really does vary, depending on the person.

The two other party members sat on the opposite side of the carriage, just a few rows down, facing back at DV-8. They travelled along in silence. He looked out of the window toward the sprawling open fields and vast forests surrounding the city. He was relieved to see they were still entirely obscured by the giant, white perimeter wall which filled the windowpane as they sped along. At least one thing was still the same as usual.

The three commuters did their best to carry on as normal and maintain minimal eye contact despite the extraordinary circumstances and the inconspicuous absence of any other party members on the train, which would usually be at capacity.

A fanfare from the train's speaker system sounded above their heads, puncturing the silence. DV-8 felt a wave of contentment crash over him at the familiar sound, and he stifled a beaming smile. Although the feeling of contentment soon dissipated when the sound was followed by an automated, recorded announcement rather than an actual broadcast from the Party leaders:

Remember – if you see anything out of the ordinary on your journey, please report it to your nearest security officer at your earliest convenience.

They couldn't help glancing around the eerily deserted carriage before fixing their gazes on the floor once again:

Also, please remember to take any personal belongings with you and surrender them to your nearest incineration unit as any non-party issued, personal belongings are strictly forbidden.

The familiar words offered only a small comfort as they echoed around the empty carriage and quickly faded away, suffocated by the resounding silence.

They neared their destination, and the silence was punctured once again. This time, an odd and almost alien sound emanated from the substantial party member sitting beside the slight woman. He was hunched over, and his shoulders rose and fell rapidly in the most peculiar manner. The man clasped one of his large hands to his face and did his best to stifle the sound as the train rolled on, but it wasn't enough to stop the inquisitive glances from his two fellow passengers. DV-8 couldn't help but stare as he realised the man's face was contorted most unusually, and the muffled, pained cries he let out echoed around the empty carriage. DV-8 could barely distinguish the few words he spoke through the gaps between his fingers and the strange sobs that intermittently overtook him.

"What are we even doing? Trying to carry on as normal...when...when...it's over! It's all over!"

DV-8 was even more puzzled when he saw the slight woman lean forward to examine the man closely with a look of grave concern. Slowly, gently she reached out to the crying man, but DV-8 was relieved when he saw that this was simply so she could lift a fold in his uniform and get a better look at his serial number: *AC-DC.* She quickly scribbled the number into her notebook to record the astonishing outburst, before quickly returning to her upright position. The sight of regular party procedure and due diligence warmed his heart. Her actions reaffirmed his hope that the bizarre events of yesterday would soon be a curious footnote in the long, successful history of The Party.

At that moment, he longed to call out and commend the brittle woman for her continued devotion to The Party, but he knew this should be saved for the commendations portion of the next weekly meeting, as was protocol. Even so, he couldn't help a slight smile as he looked on and the train pulled into the station. DV-8 and the brittle woman filed out and onto the platform in an orderly fashion.

They stopped dead as a loud, anguished cry filled the air like nothing either of them had heard before. AC-DC burst out of the train doors and raced off. DV-8 marvelled at this large barrel of a man, bounding along the platform. He didn't like to judge, but he was always disappointed to see a party member who had so neglected their health and fitness regimens, allowing themselves to become overweight. It reflected poorly on The Party as a whole. In other words, AC-DC was just a bit too heavy for his taste.

Having abandoned his attempts at stifling his sobs, AC-DC now let out a confused, atavistic wail as he disappeared through the turnstiles, ripping off his party uniform as he went.

"Down with The Party! Long live The Resistance!"

His bellowing faded as he raced off along the street outside the station.

DV-8's first instinct was to report this unprecedented incident. However, as he reached for his notebook, he realised he would have no idea how to describe such a curious outburst even if he wanted to. The sight of such unreserved, unchecked emotion in a party member was another first, and therefore another cause for concern.

He turned to leave the station but stopped as his eyes met with the brittle woman's. He saw his own confusion and concern reflected back at him. They each waited for a single breath, desperately wanting to say something, to convince each other that everything would be alright. Inwardly, they each knew that the best chance of achieving that was to continue exactly as they had before. Besides, spontaneous chatting between Party members outside of one's own department was dependent on an approved 'banter' requisition form and had to be scheduled weeks in advance.

They both *knew* the rules.

The one brief moment they shared evaporated instantly, and they filed out of the train station in an orderly fashion. The whole time DV- 8 recited silently to himself:

Keep Calm and Carry On…
Keep Calm and Carry On…
Keep Calm and Carry On…

He arrived at work disappointed to find that there was none. He checked his inbox repeatedly, hoping to find his regular update from the Senior Leadership team regarding the Supreme Leader's overseas tour but on this day, nothing. He looked around the office to see the only other two party members who had shown up for work sitting in front of their blank screens with equally blank expressions and idle hands. They, too, seemingly had received no work duties for the day.

DV-8 quickly became restless as this was a very unfamiliar sensation. He was awake, time was passing, yet he had no Party business to deal with. His days were usually heavily regimented and scheduled, so that he was never unoccupied. There was always some party task to carry out, or some pressing party business to discuss but now, there was nothing.

The empty, aimless seconds ticked by without anything to fill them; the seconds dragged into minutes with nothing assigned to them. He watched the clock tick by and marvelled at this strange phenomenon – time with nothing to fill it.

Free time?

He looked around for some instruction, some direction, anything to break up the monotony of this *free time*. He was relieved when he saw the tiny blinking light on his electronic notebook, reminding him that the memory card was full, and it would need replacing after his eventful nightly patrol the previous evening. Finally, he had a task. Something to fill the hollow space of time, time which would usually be spent productively, working up footage for the weekly report. He crossed the office to the stationary cupboard to retrieve a new notebook. Passing the large window running the width of the building, the continuous ominous rumblings and roars came floating in from the direction of the party HQ.

DV-8 did not stop to investigate further, committed as he was to the task at hand and possibly because he could not bring himself to. He took a new electronic notebook from the large stack on the shelf in the stationary cupboard. Returning to his workstation, his gaze momentarily passed over the window, and he accidentally looked straight at the scene outside the party HQ. He stepped tentatively up to the window, drawn to it by some morbid curiosity and was barely able to process what he saw. The white flags of The Party hung torn in half across the city, flickering orange flames and black smoke resulting from fires which raged in many of the Upper Party buildings. The huge stone door of the party HQ lay shattered and crumbled on the building's front steps.

A vast crowd of Party members filled the courtyard but not in the usual, precise rows; this was a throbbing, amorphous mass of humanity swaying gently, as one, to curious rhythmic sounds. Many of the party members were not dressed in their usual white overalls but clad in all kinds of different colours and garments. The only consistent colour was the dull green of two helicopters on the roof of the party HQ; these matched the dull green trucks parked around the courtyard, encircling the crowd. Strange men threw parcels out from the vehicles into the crowd's snatching hands. There was consistency also between these men, dressed in strange military-type uniforms with confusing patterns made up of the same dull green as the trucks but mixed with other shades of green and patches of different shades of brown, all in a blurred style. These odd uniforms stood out in stark contrast against the consistently white facades of the party buildings across the city, making the men very noticeable and easy to locate. DV-8 scanned the scene, blinking in disbelief.

He noticed more and more of these soldiers patrolling the city, even standing guard around the party HQ building. So much did their uniforms cause them to stand out against their surroundings, he could only conclude that this must be the point of such an unusually coloured garment; to make them as noticeable and easily identifiable as possible should one of their number become lost and require assistance. Some Party members were waving an unusual flag with a colourful, garish pattern. It was also emblazoned on the vehicles and stitched to the arms of the soldiers' dull green uniforms. It bore little resemblance to The Party flag, with horizontal red stripes running across it and a blue square in the upper left-hand corner.

DV-8 searched desperately for a familiar sight. He noticed that the white of the usual Party flag could still be seen in the blue square but only through small gaps in the shape of stars. He had been excitedly awaiting the unveiling of the new Party flag but could hardly believe they would have gone with a design so different, and gaudy compared to the quiet dignity of the original. His eyes fell upon the throbbing crowd once again. The only reference point he could conjure up was the one time he had seen that many people gathered in one place before; the celebrations held every year on the Supreme Leader's birthday. Huge teams of Party members would perform highly choreographed routines in arenas all over the city. Each participant held a coloured placard aloft, and when they came together as a group and were viewed from above by the Senior Party Leaders in the stands, they would create giant, vibrant portraits of the Supreme Leader's face in a fitting tribute to the great man. Staring at the unorganised, disjointed swaying mass of humanity now occupying the party HQ courtyard, it was unclear exactly whose face they were trying to depict. Whoever it was, they were doing a terrible job and desperately needed the guidance of one of The Party's skilled choreographers.

Still unable to process what he was seeing, one thought managed to break through and tear him away from the bizarre and troubling sight. *I'm going to need a bigger notebook*, he concluded and headed back into the stationary cupboard.

DV-8 returned to his workstation and refreshed his inbox repeatedly for the next few hours. No work duty materialised. This free time caused his mind to wander, and he felt particularly aggrieved at the manner of the deviants' celebration outside the party HQ. They were displaying their deviance blatantly through unauthorised music and dance. This seemed to him wholly ungrateful as the Supreme Leader himself had invented music and dancing in the early part of the 31st century. He composed the first song ever recorded, 'Party Rock Anthem', a spirited ode to The Party and its continued success. Just five years later, he came up with the idea of moving one's body rhythmically in time with the music to further display one's enthusiasm and commitment to The Party.

Now, these two fantastic innovations were being employed in open defiance to The Party and seemed like an insult to the Supreme Leader himself. DV-8's blood began to boil as he sat at his desk, and the hypocrisy of their actions dawned on him. Usually, his work would be a welcome distraction from such an outrage but with nothing to occupy his wandering mind, he simply sat and seethed. As this new, dreaded *free time* was becoming unbearable, a familiar sound sent a rush of relief through him:

THE FANFARE

Along with the other two employees in the office, he leapt from his chair and raced toward the centre of the room, eager to hear the message that would explain away the unprecedented recent events. They planted their feet firmly, crossed both arms across their faces, nodded briskly and stared into the infoscreen awaiting the comforting, authoritative face of the Supreme Leader to materialise. Their arms dropped listlessly to their sides almost in unison as they were confronted once again, by the ever-smiling face of BB-01.

"Good afternoon, friends."

Their mouths dropped open, again in unison, as the camera pulled back to reveal BB-01 standing at a podium, dressed in a black uniform. Another podium to his right was occupied by a tall, imposing man in one of the dull green uniforms. As DV-8 was again trying to process what he saw, he noticed the unfamiliar, garish red, white and blue flag hanging next to the tall man.

"I would like to thank each and every one of you who helped to make this dream a reality," BB-01 continued. "The Resistance has won. We have taken control of the capital, and our movement is spreading quickly across the rest of the country."

DV-8 scowled at BB-01's friendly, amenable air. He had always found it somewhat discomforting, and now he knew why.

"I'd like to offer special thanks to the General and his men," said BB-01, gesturing to the tall man at the other podium, "who have been working with us for some time to ensure a swift transition of power and so we may all safely enjoy our newfound freedoms. Freedom of movement, freedom of thought, freedom of spee…"

"If I could stop you there for a moment," the General interjected, causing BB-01 to startle slightly. "I'd like to express how impressed we are with your movement and offer our congratulations on taking your first, bold steps toward freedom."

"Yes, well…thank you, General and…"

"We have been with you for a long time in spirit, helping your new leader here," the General continued, pointing to BB-01, "to plan the operation that has led to your freedom, and now we are glad to be here in the flesh to help you during this difficult period of transition. To guide you, to lead you, to watch you."

BB-01 eyed the General closely from his podium.

"That is, to watch over you,' the General concluded.

"Right...well, thank you, General."

BB-01 continued with his address but DV-8 was so puzzled and troubled by what he was seeing, he could no longer take in anything emitting from the screen. The screen which once offered him constant reassurance and trusted guidance. His eyes drifted up to the clock above the infoscreen, and he noticed it was almost time to begin his nightly patrol. He repeated a familiar phrase as he left the office:

Keep Calm and Carry On...

Keep Calm and Carry On...

Keep Calm and Carry On...

- VII -

DV-8 RUSHED INTO HIS APARTMENT and closed the door quickly behind him. Though not quickly enough to prevent a swirl of gritty dust from entering along with him, a common occurrence since The Party cleaning crews had all but abandoned their posts.

He scurried over to the desk on the far wall, sat down and carefully removed his electronic notebook from the pouch of his overalls. Time was, he kept the notebook in his top pocket, poking out proudly for all to see as recording infractions was one of the most respected practices a party member could carry out. However, it had been several days since what people were variously calling the uprising, the takeover, or the revolution, but which DV-8 had decided to refer to as the incident. The use of the electronic notebooks had become practically non-existent. He was almost afraid to be seen using it and did so only in the privacy of his apartment, as if it were an act of deviance in itself.

Some had even taken to destroying their electronic notebooks in brazen acts of defiance against The Party. They tried burning them but found this was not the most efficient technique as they didn't catch fire as readily as traditional paper books. Eventually, they realised that the e-notebooks were not waterproof, and that water caused them to short-circuit and shut down permanently. Ever since, Resistance members had organised a mass "book-dousing" across the city, during which the e-notebooks would be piled together and sprayed down with water until their circuits fried.

DV-8 now used his notebook not only to record infractions and accusations, but as a journal for documenting as much of the bizarre goings-on since the incident as he could. Still hopeful of the Supreme Leader's return and The Party's reinstatement to power, he wanted to be helpful and have a comprehensive report ready to present to them. Before he started writing, he glanced up to ensure he was visible to the camera lens just above the infoscreen. If Party members were still monitoring them as he hoped, he wanted them to see his vigilance and diligence were as strong as ever. He started scribbling away, trying to make sense of recent events in his own mind just as much as for any future report:

It is difficult to say how long it has been since the mass delirium took hold of so many of my fellow party members. Almost all the digital clocks and calendars throughout the city have fallen into disrepair, work schedules have been abandoned, and the daily reports are no longer broadcast. All of which is apparently of no concern to anyone else but me. I approached one of my former brothers in the street to try and ascertain the correct date and time. His response of, 'What even is time, man? It's just like, a construct', I found unhelpful. He was dressed in the multi-coloured, oversized smocks that many seem to have adopted as their uniform and accompanied by a vague smell of the strange herb that I have witnessed many igniting and ingesting ever since the delirium took root among the populace. As far as I can tell, his unintelligible response is a symptom of something called, 'Free Speech', a tenet of the teachings of 'The Resistance'. This is one of the more alarming symptoms I have witnessed, and one which may drive me to delirium myself if I am subjected to it for much longer. While conversations between party members used to be productive, focused and exclusively concerned with forwarding the excellent work of The Party, this 'Free Speech' seems to come in two distinct forms. The first is the perplexing, pointless rambling I have mentioned, and the second is the incredibly mundane and repetitive.

I have kept a log of my conversations with those affected, and in the past week alone, I have been forced to endure sixteen conversations about the weather. It seems the delirium brings about a curious fascination in people for how much the weather on any given day conforms to the expected climate for the time of year: 'Hot one today!', 'Looks like rain!', 'Can you believe this weather?', 'Freezing, innit?'. These stock phrases are ubiquitous among those affected, and the victims repeat them endlessly when interacting in almost any social or professional capacity. Ironically enough, now that speech *is 'Free', I repeatedly find myself engaged in conversations I wish weren't allowed. Occasionally, I have passed some rallies that have sprung up across the city and heard speakers celebrating our newfound 'freedom of expression' from their podiums. I am confident that these speakers must not have had any actual conversations with the members of the crowds gathered before them. If they had, I'm sure, like me, they would see that the problem with people being free to speak their minds is that you find out what people are really thinking –*

DV-8 stopped writing. His hand ached with cramp, but this isn't why he stopped, he was used to powering through the pain to complete any work for The Party. He stopped only because he didn't want to be late for his nightly patrol, which he had continued to conduct fastidiously ever since the incident.

He began his patrol at the stroke of nineteen and seven minutes just as he always had. He theorised that it was now more important than ever to record all instances of deviance ready to present to the Supreme Leader upon his return when the test was over. He had decided the current events, The Resistance takeover, The Party's apparent total absence and abandonment of their people, must all be a part of some test to flush out deviants and members of The Resistance.

After all, The Party had experimented with testing the resolve and commitment of Party members in the past.

Senior Leaders would, on occasion, be sent to infiltrate certain districts, workplaces or committees and masquerade as members of The Resistance. They would secretly approach anyone they suspected and attempt to convert them to their fake cause, denouncing The Party and the Supreme Leader in the process. This practice was hurriedly discontinued when it became apparent that every Senior Leader attempting to tempt Party members to join The Resistance had a 100% success rate, inadvertently increasing support for The Resistance to the highest levels anyone had ever known. It took years to round up all Party members who had succumbed to the fake offers to join The Resistance and for support of the movement to die down once again. DV-8 was surprised to see such a test being carried out on such a grand scale but resolved to pass it and reap the rewards upon the Supreme Leader's glorious return.

He hurried along the street, head down, conscientiously carrying out his nightly patrol and noting the myriad infractions he encountered. As he rounded the corner, he was abruptly stopped and knocked to the ground. He looked up to the source of the assault and saw two Party members, arm in arm, towering over him.

"Whoops, sorry, brother!" the male party member blurted out.

The accompanying female party member gave him a cautionary frown, and a swift elbow to the side. He quickly corrected himself.

"Er…I mean, pal."

It struck DV-8, just after they had, that neither of them were wearing the white overalls of The Party. Instead, they wore trousers of a strange, coarse blue material and black T-shirts emblazoned with a gaudy pattern consisting of an eagle and the same flag he had seen dotted around the crowd outside the party HQ.

"Didn't see you there, here let me…" The man reached down toward DV-8.

DV-8 took this as a follow-up attack; he recoiled from them and scrambled to his feet. He looked back at the man in astonishment, who chuckled nervously. "Bit chilly tonight, innit mate?"

DV-8's scowl hardened in response.

"You kept the uniform?" The woman laughed as she swigged from a brown glass bottle.

"You know they're handing out clothes outside the old headquarters if you…" The man tailed off as he noticed with curiosity that DV-8 had begun scribbling away in his electronic notebook. DV-8 clasped his arms in front of his face, performing the party salute. Startled, they did not reciprocate in kind.

"I'm afraid I'm going to have to report you both," he warned as authoritatively as possible, still trying to collect himself.

Instinctively DV-8 leaned forward to inspect the front of the man's overalls but found no serial number on the unusual, short-sleeved garment he was wearing. He quickly turned to ascertain the woman's serial number, but her garment was cut so low he found himself staring directly at her exposed cleavage. He jerked back quickly as the pair watched him with growing concern.

"Could you please provide me with your serial numbers?" DV-8 asked, looking up to the sky.

"Is he serious?" She draped her arm around her partner and peered at DV-8 with narrowed eyes.

"Your serial numbers, please!" he demanded again, now looking down at the ground.

"Nobody's still using their serial numbers, pal!" the man replied as DV-8 looked everywhere except at the woman's chest again.

"Yeah, isn't it great! You get to choose whatever name you want now! Imagine the possibilities!" she exclaimed in between swigs.

"I'm John."

"And I'm Jane!"

"Jane?" DV-8 struggled to recreate the unusual sound she had offered by way of a name.

"Yeah! Jane Doe. You like it? It's very popular with the newcomers. I heard one soldier say he had already taken out five Jane Doe's since he got here!"

"What's your name?" John asked, reaching out and offering a handshake to DV-8.

"My serial number is D-V..." he replied, drawing back from him. They burst out laughing. DV-8 winced; never had he heard such a spontaneous, piercing sound.

"No! You have to pick a new one!" John insisted.

"Let's see," Jane garbled as she drunkenly leant forward and ran her fingers along DV-8's badge. "D-V...D-V...Dave!"

He drew back once again at her bizarre, unintelligible outburst.

"Dave?" her partner asked.

"Yeah! I heard it from one of the new guys the other day. Nice, right?"

"Dave...yeah, I like it. It's a bit exotic."

"I think it suits him. What do you think, Dave?"

They both turned to DV-8. He stared back dumbfounded, barely able to comprehend what they were saying. He felt a great sadness as he realised how far gone many of his fellow party members must be and resolved to help every last one by reporting them for re-education the second the Supreme Leader returned.

"I'm afraid I'll have to report you both, and when the Supreme Leader returns, he..."

DV-8 winced as their cackling pierced his eardrums.

"Yeah, ok, pal! *When* he returns!" John laughed as he took Jane by the hand and pushed past DV-8.

He watched them walk off along the street. He felt sorry that he was unable to reason with them but happy to hear their incessant cackling dying away as they disappeared into the shadows.

"See ya, Dave!" Jane shouted back.

Poor fools, DV-8 thought to himself as he watched them walk away, arm in arm, laughing at nothing in particular. He had no problem with laughter per se. He enjoyed hearing laughter from a crowd for example, whenever he was asked to add canned laughter to the Supreme Leader's speeches. This occurred on those odd occasions when the microphones present had somehow not picked up the crowd's riotous response to one of the SL's classic zingers. He also used to enjoy the annual roast that was held on the Supreme Leader's birthday, although this hadn't happened for the last few years. One year, following a particularly raucous roast, all of the roasters had disappeared on the way back to their hotels; in circumstances as mysterious as they were completely unrelated, according to the official reports. DV theorised that party members were reluctant to volunteer to participate in the event ever since, probably out of respect for the missing party members. But Jane and John's laughter was so casual, inexplicable, and aimless that it was a surefire sign they had fallen into the grips of deviation. With a tut and a sympathetic shake of his head, DV tried his best to note down the weird names they had provided in the serial number column on his electronic notebook:

J0-N and J4N3

The next mourning, the train platform was even emptier than the day before. DV-8 stood at the platform edge, waiting patiently for his usual train. The only other person waiting, at the far end of the platform, was the slight, brittle woman and he found himself strangely comforted by her presence.

He shifted uncomfortably in his now well-worn and unclean uniform. This was an unfamiliar sensation since each apartment in the city was fitted with a small compartment built into the wall where party members would place their overalls at the end of each day. The compartment was hooked up to the district plumbing system and every night would fill with water and detergent, ensuring the party uniform was ready for the next day's work. These were known as 'water closets'. The overalls would then be dried and pressed by a robotic clothes press, as good as new and ready for the next day's work. The press was free of charge to all Party members, a complimentary service the Supreme Leader felt strongly about providing. When he first announced the service being brought in, he proclaimed, 'A free press is one of the most important tenets of any successful society'. The announcement was made in the state-run *Party Gazette* which, incidentally, was the only news outlet allowed to operate under Party rule. Unfortunately, when DV-8 went to retrieve his overalls from the WC, that mourning, no cleaning had taken place, and the water closets were seemingly no longer in operation.

Even the free press had been shut down.

A worrying sign indeed.

He shifted uncomfortably again, hoping he was far enough away from the brittle woman that she could not see the dirt staining the back of his uniform from his fall the previous night. He allowed himself another glance and saw that she was eyeing him suspiciously; he was terrified she would notice the state of his uniform and report him for such an infraction but almost hoped that she would, just so he could know there was still one sane person left in the whole district.

He resumed facing forward and noticed, aptly enough from the notice board, that he had just missed his train by a few minutes. It appeared that the trains had now been scheduled to arrive on the hour by whoever was now in charge, which seemed extraordinary to DV-8. Scheduling anything on the hour had been abolished years ago by the Supreme Leader during the time reforms. Everything (train timetables, work schedules, patrol start times) was set to start at a different minute past the hour. Every quarter these times would be revised, randomised, and published in the quarterly report for Party members to check and memorise. This stopped things from getting boring, helped keep the mind active and weeded out Party members with weaker memories or poor attention to detail. How would DV ever remember that trains now ran on the hour? How very inconvenient, he thought to himself. The Supreme Leader and his team would be furious if he could see this sorry state of affairs. In fact, the reliability and efficiency of the public transport system was something the senior leaders took great pride in.

He remembered when he was young, Party leaflets would often be posted out to all households keeping everyone up to date with Party business. One of the first ones he remembered seeing read:

> *The Supreme Leader has indeed enjoyed many great and important successes during his time in charge; he may have eradicated deviance in almost all districts; he may have re-educated and rehabilitated all citizens who have succumbed to deviance, but he also takes care of the party member in the street. Say as many wonderful things as you like about the Supreme Leader but don't forget he also makes the trains run on time.*

It was something that DV-8 had begun to take for granted, and he felt the guilt and shame wash over him now that his train was late for the first time in his life. Maybe, he thought, this was another reason for the odd happenings of late. This test that the Supreme Leader was putting them through. Perhaps it was also a way to emphasise how good life was under his rule. To get everyone to stop taking him for granted and be more appreciative of his Supreme Leadership. DV smiled at the ingenuity of the Supreme Leader. Good old SL was still teaching him valuable lessons despite his supposed absence. He looked forward more than ever to his glorious return but worried now that maybe this would only happen if they could somehow show they had learned their lesson and convey their renewed appreciation and devotion to him.

But how?

When he finally stopped daydreaming about the Supreme Leader's return and the restoration of Party rule, he noticed with dread that the next train still wouldn't be arriving for another fifty-six minutes. This meant he would be late for work for the first time in his life. Not a good look if he wanted to show his renewed devotion and appreciation of the Supreme Leader; he was sure that work attendance, patrol hours and the like were still being monitored through the cameras on the infoscreens as part of the test.

He pondered on what to do. He had only ever taken the train to work as this was the only authorised mode of commuting. The Party liked to keep the streets as clear as possible to avoid what used to be referred to as the dreaded 'rush hour'. Roads and sidewalks were only permitted for use by Senior Leadership team members in the mournings. He weighed up what would constitute a worse infraction in his mind, being late for work or using the sidewalks without authorisation. He shifted uncomfortably in his increasingly soiled overalls once again and felt as if his mind shifted uncomfortably inside his head at the same time. This was an unfamiliar sensation that he was not used to at all – making a decision for himself.

He glanced along the platform and saw the woman look from the clock across the platform and over to him. Her expression remained fixed, but her eyes pulsed with fear. He watched as she squinted and squirmed, obviously wrestling with the same strange sensation he was feeling and looking for guidance, but what was to be done? He had seen that pleading in her eyes somewhere before: the face of his old roommate DV-9 flashed through his mind at the instant he had pressed the red button and summoned the security officers to collect her.

Before he had logically reached a decision for himself, almost in a panicked attempt to alleviate the discomfort he saw in the slight woman's eyes, DV-8 found himself taking a tentative step back away from the edge of the platform and towards the exit. He stopped, astonished at the effect her look of dismay had on him and surprised by his own action. He glanced furtively along the platform and was strangely pleased when he saw her follow his lead and take a small, unsure step back from the platform. Emboldened by her response, he took another step back and waited. After a moment, she reciprocated in kind once again. He continued slowly, and she followed at an even slower pace. Before he knew it, DV-8 spun on his heel and marched out of the station and she did the same. They emerged onto the street at the same time and looked at one another. Their eyes met for a moment, but before any thought or feeling could be conveyed, they each span and marched off in opposite directions towards their workplaces, equally determined not to be late.

As he walked away, DV-8's only hope was that she didn't turn around and notice how dirty the back of his uniform was. Luckily, his backpack somewhat obscured her view, which he carried in order to transport the dozens of electronic notebooks he had filled in the preceding night's patrol.

The streets were empty, calm, and sterile. As a humble lower party member, DV-8 lived and worked on the outskirts of the city, and the continuing deviant celebrations seemed to be confined to the city centre. For the time being, at least.

Unfortunately, while he did both live and work on the outskirts of the city; the outskirts in which he lived were on the opposite side of the city to the outskirts in which he worked, so he had quite the journey ahead of him. Walking along the towering city perimeter wall, he could no longer hear the ominous rumblings coming from the party HQ as he was too far away. There was no sign of the widespread looting, arson, and destruction of property that he had encountered on his nightly patrols. No strung-up effigies of the Supreme Leader, no strangely coloured flags, no symbols of The Resistance daubed onto walls and screens. For a few moments, he could forget the troubling recent events and convince himself that nothing had happened, that everything was just as it was, as it should be and will surely be again someday soon.

He was torn from his comforting daydreams by a loud clanging sound, metal on metal. He looked up to the top of a staircase affixed to the perimeter wall, which led to a robust steel door. He watched as the warm mourning breeze eased the unlocked door open, then slammed it back with a bang. He watched the process repeat over and over. He had never seen a door to the perimeter wall open before. They were permanently locked and had been for as long as he could remember. He pouted at yet another reminder of how things had changed, how standards had slipped so dramatically, and how many Party members now completely neglected their responsibilities.

So offended was he that, despite knowing he was no longer a member of the perimeter wall maintenance committee or any of its eight subcommittees and it was entirely out of his jurisdiction, he began climbing the metal staircase, determined to put at least this one infraction right, immediately.

He stomped to the top of the staircase and gripped the handle but before forcing the door closed, he stopped. His anger subsided, and his boiling blood was reduced to a simmer as he gently pulled the door open and stared out in dumbstruck amazement. A wide, open space carpeted with verdant green and overlooked by a canopy of deep, rich blue. Flashes of yellow and red buds punctuated the green while white brushstrokes intermittently swept across the blue canvas. The only sound was the gentle rustling of the breeze passing through a solitary, noble oak tree, and the fragrant aromas of nature filled his nostrils. It was a sight like nothing he had ever seen. It filled all his senses at once, overwhelmed them and consumed him. The world behind him: the city, the trains, and the office buildings seemed to melt away to nothing. He felt strangely drawn to this new world and inhaled the warm, sweetly scented air that caressed his face.

His bottom lip began to quiver.

He slammed the door shut with a bang and wrenched the lock back into place with a dull metallic thud, sealing off the mystifying scene, safely behind the wall. He was unsure what he had seen but knew that he wanted things back the way they were, and whatever lay beyond the wall was even more alien to him than the city had become. With the door securely locked, he stomped back down the staircase, determined to make it to work on time and to prove his unwavering devotion to the Supreme Leader, certain that he would reap the rewards upon his glorious return.

He marched hurriedly along the street and turned the corner quickly but soon found he was forced to stop and record yet another infraction. He saw a man lying prostrate on the pavement, brown glass bottles strewn all around him. DV-8 started scribbling away in his notebook.

"Hey! What are you doing?" the man garbled as he rolled over onto his back.

DV-8 looked up, their eyes met, and he was surprised to see it was AC-DC, the portly man from the train, the one he had caught crying, or was it laughing? He was obviously drunk and dressed even more strangely than the couple he had encountered yesterday. He wore the same trousers of a coarse, blue material but his were tightly wrapped around his legs and barely contained his generous proportions. His white T-shirt was stretched almost to breaking point and emblazoned with a curious slogan in black typeface: The letter 'I', then a red heart symbol and underneath the letters 'N' and 'Y'. DV-8 could only wonder who this I-NY was and what impressive feats of productivity or obedience he had performed for The Party that they would produce such a laudatory slogan and garment in his honour.

"I'm afraid I'll have to report you brother."

"But we can do what we want now...so you can't do that!" AC-DC tried to raise himself but collapsed in a drunken heap.

"And is this..." DV-8 looked down with pity at the drunken man and the detritus strewn around him, "...is this what you want, brother?"

"Must be," he replied, scanning his stark surroundings. "I'm doing it."

AC-DC raised one of the half-empty bottles to his lips. DV-8 was shocked at how far his comrade had fallen in such a short time. He knew he had to do something to help his confused fellow Party member, so he promptly finished recording the infraction. Unfortunately, he could not deny that if this all was a test, many of his fellow Party members were currently failing miserably.

- VIII -

DV-8 WAS GLAD HE HAD hurried and was relieved to arrive at work just in time, only to find that, once again, there were no work assignments for the day. The office was now completely unoccupied except for him, but he remained at his station for the duration of the workday. After the first few hours, once he was sure no work orders were forthcoming, he took out his notebook. He began scribbling away in his journal once again. Periodically, he smiled up into the camera above the infoscreen, safe in the knowledge his commitment and diligence would be recorded for future prosperity:

> *Along with this curious obsession with Free Speech, the delirium also seems to induce a severe lethargy in its victims which the Resistance has rebranded as a positive attribute; they call it 'Free Time'. The majority of my former brothers and sisters have elected to completely abandon their posts and spend their days congregating at the endless street parties that have all but taken over the city. Even those whose minds seem less affected and who are seemingly still able to work have been co-opted into*

carrying out the pointless, menial tasks deemed necessary by the Resistance.

A few days ago, I happened into one of the curious 'cafes' that have popped up all over the city. Many people now congregate here in the service of nothing but passing their 'free time'. There I saw one of my former sisters, an engineer of some description, who once would have carried out important work in one of the party foundries or arms factories. I was heartened to see how diligently and expertly she worked away at the large, complex contraption behind the counter and the evident innovation it must have taken to construct such a machine with its numerous levers, dials and switches. But whereas before, her expertise, knowledge and hard work would have served to keep the national grid in working order or to produce arms for the war effort, all she now produced was a warm, brown liquid which dripped from the remarkable machine. She then poured it into cups to be ingested by the reclining patrons. To a man, they all remained apathetic and completely oblivious to the hard work that went into its preparation.

This curious concoction seemed to serve no purpose but to fuel the incessant 'free speech' that once again began to fill the small space, rendering it unbearable and forcing me to take my leave. I fear the effect that this complete lack of coherent conversation and meaningful work is having on my mental state as well as that of my former comrades. They display a total rejection of all established hierarchies and the proper orders of society. Authority is no longer granted based on hereditary peerage but to those with the vision and fortitude to command respect amongst their fellow man. Platforms are no longer granted to those in high office but to those with something to say and the charisma to captivate an audience. Partners are no longer assigned to each other but chosen on personal preference, with the distinct advantage given to the considerate, the personable and the charming.

In a word, chaos.

But what of the common man born without such natural talents and gifts? Will we now be expected to develop these skills within ourselves? To address and overcome our shortcomings? To self-reflect and self-improve? Ridiculous! This complete inequality of opportunity strikes me as wholly unjust. It can lead only to a future of accountability, introspection, consideration of others and a complete overhaul of the systems and structures that make up our society. That sounds like a lot of hard work to me and I, for one, will not stand for such a bleak and hellish future. I fear, however, that any alternative becomes less likely by the day.

My only hope is that there are others out there like me, others who have not yet succumbed to the delirium and that there may be one who could help the people realise the error of their ways. To show them that the way of The Party must endure, to return to a time when everything was precise and certain. To overcome their affliction and to deviate from the dangerous path they are now on –

The next showing of *The Film* was scheduled for that evening, and as the workday ended, DV-8 hoped against hope that this was one part of the usual schedule that would remain intact. Surely, he thought, people couldn't have lost their minds to the point where they no longer wanted to see the same film they have watched at the same time every week since they were children.

He was late arriving at the theatre, pausing outside to record his own tardiness as an infraction in his e-notebook. Unfortunately, this made him another couple of minutes late, and he would need to add this further infraction later when he found the chance.

He rushed inside, and to his delight, he could hear the film playing in the auditorium and see the shining light of the projector through the glass windows on the doors. He gasped with excitement; they hadn't completely lost their minds. He made his way inside but was immediately halted and drew back from the deafening noise emanating from the giant screen, a cacophonic assault of explosions, gunfire, screaming, and yelling. He looked up at the screen but had to quickly shield his eyes from the rapid flashes of colour and light. It was certainly a film, but it most definitely was not *The Film*.

He squinted and tried to adjust to what he was seeing on the screen. A bizarre, chaotic mix of images spliced together and played in quick, dizzying succession; a small band of fighters in garish, colourful spandex masks and uniforms, a monstrous purple creature roaring, a maddening frenzy of laser fire and constant, brain-rattling explosions. He shielded his eyes and was forced to look away but what he saw then was even more alarming; rows and rows of people, his former comrades, gawping brainlessly at the screen, mouths open, enthralled by what they were watching.

Not a Party uniform in sight.

The ear-splitting noise and blinding flashes of colour became too much. He could barely take in anything else around him but caught worrying glimpses wherever he looked; people scoffing popcorn, people with their arms around each other, people cheering on the incomprehensible action on the screen. DV-8 grabbed for his notebook but quickly realised it was no use. He could not stand being inside the auditorium for another second and raced back out into the foyer.

In the front row, sat next to the General, was BB-01. He sensed the commotion from the back of the room and looked but was too late to see DV-8 rushing out. The

General nudged him with the point of his elbow and directed him back towards the screen with a triumphant grin.

"Pretty great, huh?"

BB-01 struggled to hear him over the deafening noise pouring out of the screen but smiled politely and settled back into his chair to try and enjoy the rest of the film.

DV-8 staggered back out into the street. The seriousness of the situation was beginning to settle in.

IF people could enjoy watching THAT, they have truly lost their minds, he thought to himself.

It was all well and good for the Supreme Leader to put his people to the test, but at this rate, there would be no sane party members left by the time of his glorious return.

As DV-8 was beginning to despair, he looked up and was relieved to see a man in Party uniform approaching from the other end of the street. He smiled to himself watching him diligently scribbling away in his notebook, examining the destruction, vandalism and litter, which was becoming more ever-present by the day. The man looked up and they locked eyes. They both heaved a sigh of relief in almost perfect unison.

DV-8 went to approach but swiftly faltered; he watched cautiously as a small group of people approached the man. Reassuringly, the group was made up of two men in the black uniforms of the security department. Worryingly, they were joined by two other men wearing the strange dull, green uniforms he had seen the day before with the brash red, white and blue flag emblazoned on the sleeves. He was too far away to hear the conversation, but the way they menacingly surrounded the man was enough to give him fair warning. DV-8 retreated into a back alley and watched from a safe distance; one of the dull green soldiers callously slapped the notebook out of the man's hands. As he bent down to retrieve his notebook, one of the security officers pushed him to the ground and their mocking laughter filled the air. The other dull green soldier and the other security officer hooked the man under each arm and started to drag him away. The man's eyes met DV-8's. They were filled with panic and pleading for help. DV-9's face flashed through his mind again; the same helplessness, the same desperation, the same horror. DV-8 turned and marched off purposefully in the opposite direction. Of course, he wanted to help his comrade, but on the other hand, he didn't want to be late for the weekly meeting.

He reached the meeting hall more concerned than ever; even the security officers had succumbed to deviance and were failing the Supreme Leader's test. And just who were these soldiers in dull green seemingly aiding The Resistance and driving the push for mass deviance? Were the General and BB-01 part of the test, or were they taking advantage of the Supreme Leader's absence to further their own agendas?

DV-8 was glad to have the regular weekly meeting to distract him from his ever-growing concerns. He was not surprised to find the meeting hall empty, but he looked up into the camera above the lifeless infoscreen and felt safe knowing that his commitment would be recorded as part of the test and rewarded later. He placed his huge stack of electronic notebooks down on one of the chairs in the front row and sat down: he was early, so he sat and waited in silence for twenty-seven minutes. The second the clock on the wall struck twenty-nine past the hour, that month's weekly meeting start time, he sprang to his feet.

"Serial number D-V Eight. All nightly patrols conducted. Two hundred and eighteen acts of deviance to report. One hundred and twelve accusations to make at this time."

He picked up the first electronic notebook from the pile and began scrolling through it.

"Incident number one," he began.

"…Accusation number one hundred and twelve. Serial number A-C-D-C."

DV-8 cleared his throat. His voice had become strained and his throat sore from just over two hours of uninterrupted reporting; it was the happiest he had been since the incident.

"Observed crying, or maybe it was laughing. Possibly both, whatever the exact circumstances, re-education would be recommended." He placed the last notebook back on the pile, nodded toward the camera above the infoscreen, and collapsed into his chair. With his report over, the silence of the cavernous meeting hall engulfed him. He looked dead ahead into the infoscreen's deep black sheen. The same infoscreen that had always provided him with answers; what to do, where to go, how to act was now blank and silent. He yearned once more for it to provide him with guidance, for some instruction on handling the worrying recent events.

Nothing.

Slowly, he approached and placed a tentative hand onto the smooth black surface, imploring it to light up, to bleat out the familiar fanfare and provide him with some answers.

No response.

His head dropped, and a defeated sigh passed his lips.

"Excuse me, brother."

DV-8's head snapped back up, and in the screen's reflection, he saw the slight, brittle woman approaching from the meeting hall entrance. He spun around to face her. Relieved to see the party uniform, relieved to see the stack of electronic notebooks under her arm, relieved to see her.

"Yes, sister?"

DV-8 crossed his arms across his face and nodded, performing the party salute. She reciprocated in kind.

"Viva la Institution!" she exclaimed.

This slightly outdated slogan had once been a mandatory retort meant to accompany the party salute whenever it was performed; a holdover from the days when the ruling class was known as *The Institution,* before their rebranding as The

Party. The change was designed to show the hip, cooler, more fun side of the authoritarian dictatorship. These days the slogan was used only by the most committed members who often secretly felt 'Party' was a touch too jovial. DV was glad to hear it and enthusiastically reciprocated in kind. The rebrand was also essential for pushing the Supreme Leader's new anti-individuality agenda which was to be heralded by a new slogan, 'There is no 'I' in 'The Party'. The Supreme Leader was very keen on this slogan, and it just wouldn't have worked without the rebrand since, as a few of the senior leaders had to tactfully point out to him, there are in fact several I's in *The Institution*.

"Forgive me, brother," she said, nervously edging toward him from the back of the meeting hall, "my district's weekly meeting was not attended by any other party members. I was hoping I could join this meeting, if possible?"

"Of course, sister," he replied, trying to temper his surprise and delight in seeing another Party member still carrying out their regular duties. "I have finished my report, but please…"

He motioned to the rows and rows of empty chairs. She took a seat on the back row, he returned to his seat, and they sat in silence for a moment.

"Serial number Ten C-C," she barked as she sprang up to her feet. "All nightly patrols conducted. One hundred and seventy-eight acts of deviance to report. Eighty-four accusations to make at this time."

DV-8 stared straight ahead into the infoscreen but now didn't feel engulfed by the stark blackness of the smooth, empty surface staring back at him; his eyes fell on the reflection of 10- CC stood to attention at the back of the room. A slight smile crept into the corners of his mouth.

"Incident number one," she began.

Seventy-six minutes later, they filed out of the meeting hall in single file, as was procedure. 10-CC turned in the direction of her district.

"Er, sister?" The words escaped DV-8's lips before he even knew why.

She halted, confused. There was no further Party business to discuss as best she could tell.

"Feel free to join the meeting again next week, if your district's is still not...so well attended."

"Thank you, brother." She winced at the curious way the corners of her mouth angled upwards upon hearing his invitation. It was a peculiar sensation.

They stood in silence for a moment facing one another. DV-8 cleared his throat to speak but faltered as it dawned on him that there was nothing to say. He had never had this problem before. He used to enjoy chatting with his fellow party members. However, with no work duties to speak of, no weekly report to discuss and all party business seemingly suspended, it was difficult to know what to say when there was nothing to talk about. He looked up at her and saw the pleading in her eyes once again, the same pleading he saw in the eyes of the man accosted outside the theatre, the same pleading he saw in the eyes of DV-9. He longed to say something to appease them but still nothing came to mind.

"Troubling times, eh brother?"

She punctured the silence with a few softly spoken words, and the joy they brought to DV-8 was resounding. Before he knew it, they were both chatting away with great energy and urgency. It brought to mind the excitement he used to feel when discussing quarterly reports, munitions production data or the seasonal crop yields of the various districts. He was relieved to find that she was as baffled as he was by the recent behaviour of their fellow Party members.

"I mean, what are they even rebelling against? What was wrong with the way things were?"

"I'm not even sure they know themselves," he answered. "I accidentally stumbled upon a copy of their manifesto".

"Really? What did it say?"

"Lots of oppression this and subjugation that."

"Absurd!" she blurted, personally offended.

"Oh yes, you should be more upset than anyone, sister," he said sarcastically, "apparently women especially are subject to the harshest discrimination: wealth inequality, harassment, mansplaining!"

"Ha! So, a man simply explaining something to me is discrimination now, is it?"

"Actually," he interrupted, "it's only technically mansplaining if the concept being explained is relatively simple and already understood by the female in question. The explanation must be delivered in a patronising tone for it to qualify. Does that make sense?"

"Yes, well…"

"Patronising means to talk down to or to treat someone as if they are not very bright," he concluded.

"Right. Anyway…"

They talked long into the evening. Each expressed their concern with the recent events; The Resistance seemingly taking over, the lack of communication from The Party and the Supreme Leader, the strange soldiers patrolling the streets and the unusual broadcast from BB-01. She agreed that it must all be part of some kind of test by the Supreme Leader and the Senior Leadership Team and shared his concerns that so many seemed to be failing and succumbing to deviance on a scale larger than they had ever seen before.

"If only there were something we could do to help," she said, "To remind everyone of the Supreme Leader's supreme leadership and how good we had it before."

They fell into reminiscing about life before the incident, failing to notice that the nightly curfew was fast approaching. DV-8 spoke about his work in the News Department, and his eyes shone with a pride and passion that had been missing ever since all the unpleasantness began. She told him about her work in the Broadcast Department and how disconcerting it was to no longer have any work to do. There had been no footage to broadcast or directives from The Party in what felt like years, but in reality, had been little more than a week. They shared everything they were both missing about regular Party-life: the meetings, the reports, the seminars on deviance suppression, *The Film* screenings, and *The Book* clubs. They each lamented that they now may never be chosen to take part in the biennial 'Hunger Games'. The Hunger Games took place on a remote island just off the mainland and not much was known about what went on, only that to be chosen to take part was an extremely high privilege. As far as DV-8 knew, every other year a select few party members were chosen to take part in a series of fun challenges and activities all to raise money for the party food drive. Some high-profile Party members were initially critical of the scheme as it so closely resembled a project that the Japanese government had put in place at least a decade earlier. The similarities were so obvious that some of these high-profile Party members couldn't believe that anyone would buy it as an original Party policy and were outspoken in their criticisms, even going so far as to call it a total rip-off of the Japanese original. Coincidentally, these were the same Party members chosen to take part the following year and what they saw must have been very convincing as they never once raised their concerns again, or indeed spoke or appeared publicly in any capacity whatsoever.

10-CC even reminded him of things he had almost forgotten, like the Replenishment Ceremonies. These took place around once a year ever since it was forecast that the birth rate was at risk of falling under optimum replacement levels. Many people advocated subsidising pregnancy care and childcare costs for all to tackle the declining birth rates, but the Supreme Leader was, as usual, the voice of reason. He decided these methods would be too expensive and a detriment to Party members in the long run. He designed a more elegant solution by completely banning abortions and instituting the Replenishment Ceremonies. Two Party members would be assigned to one another and for the entirety of the Conjugal Day public holiday were encouraged to *conjugulate* as many times as possible in twenty-four hours. It was one of the routine Party duties that interested DV-8 least, but right now he would welcome any return to normality he could get.

"Maybe we could do it ourselves, brother! Together!" she exclaimed.

"Sister?" he retorted loudly, taken aback by what she seemed to be suggesting.

"Between us, maybe we could find a way to reach out to people, remind them how good they had it before. Bring them back to their senses."

"Oh, I see," he sighed, relieved.

"You said you have some footage you were working on for the next weekly report, yes?"

He looked into her eyes and was relieved to see the pleading desperation had dissipated but was anxious about the burning excitement now causing them to twinkle back at him. They still wanted something from him, but he couldn't be entirely sure what it was exactly. It was no longer help but something different – camaraderie, collaboration, companionship? All of these were generally frowned upon by The Party, but these were unprecedented times after all.

"Ah yes, but…er…" he stumbled.

"Well, the broadcast system remains operational, brother, and I have the access. It may help remind people of the glory and wisdom of the Supreme Leader and the fight against deviance we've all worked so hard for."

"It's certainly an interesting idea." He contemplated her words carefully. "And perhaps if the Supreme Leader witnesses people coming to their senses, their renewed devotion, he may deem us worthy of his return sooner rather than later."

"Exactly, brother!"

Her eyes lit up, still inducing anxiety in him but it was now also mixed with something else, a more unfamiliar emotion – excitement, enthusiasm, hope?

Finally, they noticed that the nightly curfew was fast approaching, and made hurried arrangements for the following day. 10-CC crossed her arms in front of her face, performing the party salute. He reciprocated in kind.

"Goodnight, Sister," he remarked just as she went to leave.

She looked back at him with slightly narrowed eyes, "Goodnight…brother."

They spun and headed off in opposite directions.

On her walk home, 10-CC took out her electronic notebook and scribbled DV-8's serial number under the DEVIANTS heading. In the BEHAVIOUR column, she wrote, OVER-FAMILIARITY. However, she left the CONFIRMED column blank. Under more usual circumstances, she would not dream of giving someone a second chance or the benefit of the doubt. In fact, she had been commended in the past by Senior Leaders for her ruthless vigilance and strict enforcement of the party rules, but for now, she needed all the help she could get.

- IX -

ALTHOUGH HE STILL FELT STRANGE walking to work rather than taking the commuter train that had now seemingly ceased running, DV-8 strode through the streets with renewed energy and purpose. He had agreed on a plan with 10-CC, which calmed him as it was the closest thing to any sort of work he had for days. He would go into the News Department as usual, retrieve the footage he had already created for the upcoming weekly report, head to the Broadcast Department and hand it over to her for transmission on all the infoscreens across the city.

He had nearly reached his office when he saw yet another screen daubed with the now ever-present Resistance symbol, a giant letter 'R' with a ring around it in yellow paint. The font was much more legible than the previous graffiti he had seen. He at least had to admire the effort that had gone into the artwork and the improvement on their previous attempts. The Resistance members must have at least some work ethic and discipline, even though they managed to hide it well most of the time. He had been recording the countless instances of graffiti and resistance symbols for reporting later, upon the Supreme Leader's return; this mourning his renewed hope and passion meant that he decided to deal with the infraction himself.

Immediately.

As before, he quickly made his way to the nearest equipment shed and requested the necessary cleaning equipment and materials. After two hours of patiently waiting for a response, he gave up hope of receiving an answer. He suspected his request might go unanswered given the current circumstances, but he wanted to give them a chance to respond just in case. As he could not receive the approval of the requisite two upper party members, he completed and submitted an ECF form (*Extenuating Circumstance Form*) instead. He did his best to summarise the events of the past week on the form, but try as he might, he couldn't adequately explain within the form's strict and limited maximum word count. It took seven or eight drafts before he finally managed to produce an accurate and concise explanation:

Collapse of government/total societal revolution.

DV-8 hoped this excuse would be sufficient for bypassing the usual channels, but knowing the extenuating circumstances committee, it would be touch and go. He gave them another couple of hours and, as he half expected, received no response. Still, he was satisfied that there would be a record of his submission when the inevitable investigation occurred upon the Supreme Leader's return. After all, DV-8 knew that you couldn't be too careful in these matters. The unnecessary use of resources was a recurrent problem which The Party came down hard on. A few years ago, it was discovered the cleaning crews were using excessive amounts of water when cleaning the gates of the perimeter wall. As a result, many party members were removed from their posts and some even sent for re-education. The Water-Gate scandal, as it became known, was one of the biggest scandals ever to rock The Party and the consequences for such an infraction were still fresh in DV's mind.

He took the cleaning equipment and materials from the tool shed and returned to the offending infoscreen. Only when he climbed the step ladder and got closer to the screen did he notice that the enormous letter 'R' and the circle around it were not painted onto the screen but were being projected through it. He was relieved to find this was not another case of graffiti but felt alarmed that the Resistance were now controlling the infoscreens. Relief washed over him again as this meant the broadcast system was still up and running, so they still had a good chance of broadcasting their message. Disappointment crept in once he realised the group's penmanship had not actually improved and that any work ethic or discipline he had attributed to them, was unfounded.

It was a real emotional rollercoaster of a mourning.

Returning to the equipment shed to drop off the cleaning supplies, he couldn't get the offending symbol out of his mind. He again pondered The Resistance and their motivations for opposing The Party and the Supreme Leader's rule. He thought back to the secret book he had discovered and remembered some of the ludicrous and nonsensical ramblings contained within it. He remembered a lot of confused diatribes about how The Party was too dogmatic in its following of the Supreme Leader's teachings as if his word was the objective truth. That The Party were far too black and white in their rulings and life is much more subjective than they portrayed it as.

I'll be the judge of that, thank you very much, DV-8 thought to himself.

They claimed that The Party would psychologically torment their citizens by keeping them in a perpetual state of 'cognitive dissonance' – forcing them often to accept and believe two completely contradictory ideas as truth simultaneously. DV-8 didn't understand this idea of cognitive dissonance at all, yet at the same time, he understood it perfectly; the concept was absolutely clear to him, but he couldn't think of a single instance of The Party contradicting themselves in this way. Having returned the cleaning supplies, he made his way to work and noticed the badly damaged bus stop across the street. He remembered how the Supreme Leader's quick thinking and defusing expertise had saved them all from their enemies overseas during the last missile strike and began to miss him even more. Then he recalled that it actually wasn't their enemies overseas who had launched the attack, that it was simply a demonstration of The Party's defensive capabilities. He chuckled at his own silly mistake and couldn't think of any reason why he thought, momentarily, that it was a real attack.

Anyway, he missed the Supreme Leader all the same.

One of the more egregious statements of the group found in the secret book was that they claimed to be fighting for equality for all. DV-8 found this particularly ridiculous as The Party were famed for the equal treatment of all party members and their inclusive nature towards marginalised groups. It was The Party, after all, who decided that disabled party members were just as capable of carrying out hard labour as any other party members and encouraged them to enter the workforce and enrol in the labour camps. Even when many in the disabled community seemed to have a collective crisis of confidence and claimed they were unable to take part, The Party showed their commitment to equality and inclusion for all by giving them the extra push they needed, making their enrolment in the labour camps mandatory, just like it was for everybody else. The secret book also mentioned wanting more freedoms with less stringent laws imposed on Party members, but once again, he found this impossible to relate to. After all, The Party was not so puritanical in its law-making. For example, drugs had been legalised long ago and were permitted, even mandatory for party members in some circumstances.

The most popular drug, 'Asmo', was often prescribed to Party members who were feeling disillusioned with life under party rule or whose quality of work had shown signs of slipping. The drug would help them to relax and eradicate any unwanted deviant thoughts or, even worse, feelings. Feelings, or 'The F word' as many Party members preferred to refer to them, were something DV was yet to experience and, according to the rumours, not something he was in a hurry to experience either.

The Resistance should count themselves lucky, he thought. It could be a lot worse; he had read in history books about how past governments had dealt with drugs in society and how they were much stricter than The Party. Some had gone as far as waging what was known as a 'War on Drugs'. He scoffed as he considered what a ridiculous notion this would be. Had these people ever actually tried to do anything on drugs, let alone fight a war? The admin alone must have been a nightmare. DV-8 couldn't help but shake his head at the delusional beliefs The Resistance were operating under as he set off for the News Department.

Having downloaded the footage from his work console onto his electronic notebook, he made his way to the Broadcast Department. He found 10-CC's office to be just as empty as his own. Hers was the only occupied cubicle in the entire office. As he arrived, she stood, crossed her arms in front of her face and nodded curtly. He reciprocated in kind.

"You are four hours late, brother."

"Forgive me, sister. I was dealing with yet another instance of heinous Resistance graffiti I encountered on an infoscreen near my office."

"Oh," she smiled in admiration of his hard work and commitment, "Well, I trust you were able to resolve the situation."

"Er...yes, sort of," he stuttered. DV-8 was nervous but unsure as to why.

She raised her eyebrows inquisitively.

"Well, the infoscreen is graffiti free anyway."

"Glad to hear it, brother. Now..."

She reached forward and held out her open palm before him. Another pleading gesture, he thought to himself, and at that moment, he again wanted nothing more than to help her, but what was she looking for? Did she want him to reach out and take her hand, to reassure her that everything would be alright? Such a brazen act would of course be forbidden, but these were extraordinary times after all.

"Sister, I..."

"You did bring the footage as we agreed, didn't you?" she said, cutting him off. 10-CC narrowed her eyes at his uncomfortable shifting.

"Oh, yes, of course, sorry." He fumbled in the front pocket of his overalls with nervous, shaky hands and produced his electronic notebook.

She reached out slowly and plucked it from him with nimble fingers.

"Good work, brother."

DV-8 beamed as he sat next to 10-CC, watching the footage play out on her work console; the Supreme Leader delivering his speech at a meeting of the United Nations. He felt immediately calmed and reassured upon seeing the Supreme Leader's trademark stoic charisma and hearing his commanding, refreshingly monotone voice.

She also sat enraptured. It felt as though she hadn't seen her beloved leader for so long. She was reminded how handsome he was with his sharp, piercing features and tidy, precise haircut. It was a face that induced a feeling of stability and consistency because the Supreme Leader had worn the same clean-shaven, no-nonsense look for as long as 10-CC could remember. There was a brief period in which the SL experimented slightly with his look, sporting a small, square black moustache in the centre of his top lip for a time. She thought it quite suited him, but the slightly more hirsute look was short-lived as it turned out to have troubling connotations with a rather unsavoury historical figure. After all, the last person the Supreme Leader should be associated with is a comedian; comedy being, as we all know, a gateway to deviance. So unfortunately, the moustache had to go, and although she'd never heard of him, she had this Charlie Chaplin character to thank for it, whoever he was.

Seeing his face, DV-8 was reminded how he had long hoped to return to the days when all male Party members were required to adopt the same haircut as the Supreme Leader. Since this law was relaxed some years earlier, DV often agonised over what side to part his hair on and was never fully confident he found his signature look. It was a source of envy between him and the female Party members who were not burdened with having to expend so much time and energy thinking about their appearance as they had only one acceptable hairstyle: shoulder length, straight with the fringe stopping an inch and a quarter above the eyebrows. Simple. The Supreme Leader's speech ended, and the screen faded to black.

"Excellent work as always, brother," she said, brushing her easily manageable hair behind her ears.

"Thank you, sister," he replied, staring into the black sheen of the now blank screen on the console and somehow not seeing his reflection staring back at him, so preoccupied as he was with hers. If he had caught his reflection, he would notice that he had accidentally parted his hair on the wrong side that mourning which would cause him much distress, so it was probably best that he didn't.

"But perhaps we need to add something."

"Add something!"

DV-8 was almost offended on behalf of the Senior Leadership team, who had always provided him with clear, comprehensive instructions on creating the weekly reports from which he had never once deviated or amended.

"Well, if the footage has the desired effect and people start to come to their senses, it would be good to have some way to show The Party, the Supreme Leader even. This would prove we are passing his test and hopefully expedite his return".

"Good point, sister, but…"

"We could instruct them to come together," her words flowed faster, and her gestures became more excitable, "in a show of solidarity, a message to the Supreme Leader that we are still committed to him and ready for his return."

"Yes, well maybe."

Amending the Senior Leadership team's instructions felt almost blasphemous, but at the same time, he couldn't help but admire her enthusiasm and ingenuity.

"OK, go ahead, brother."

She re-positioned her keyboard and swivelled the screen of her work console towards him. He looked back at her with a surprised, blank expression. It was an expression she had only seen on the faces of those Party members who had decided to try The Party's trendy new health treatment – lobotomisation. That was when the procedure was in vogue a few years back.

"Add on the closing message," she smiled back at him, "then I can take it to the broadcast suite."

DV-8 shifted awkwardly in his chair and straightened up the already straightened keyboard and monitor. Resting his hands on the keyboard, he stared into the blank screen, imploring it to light up with instructions from the Senior Leadership team as it had countless times before. He took great pride in his work and was very good at bringing their written reports to life but never had he been asked to contribute any words or ideas of his own. The very thought of it felt alien and uncomfortable. He winced as his brain strained to perform an unknown function. 10-CC stared expectantly at the screen.

Nothing appeared.

As DV-8 began to straighten up the already straightened desktop for the second time, something else caught her eye – the rip on the leg of DV-8's overalls. She smiled. It was now sewn up tightly: only a slight wrinkle in the material and a millimetre of loose thread showed that there ever was a rip at all.

"You know, I have to admit, brother."

DV-8 exhaled at the sound of her voice, glad of any distraction from his impossible task.

"That day on the train," she continued, still staring at the sewn rip, "when I observed the rip in your overalls."

He followed her gaze and cringed with embarrassment at the sight of the rip.

"I was worried that you were just like the rest of them."

He looked up and saw she was now facing him. He saw a glimmer of light had returned to her eyes.

"But now I know, you are so much more."

The pleading in her eyes had been replaced by hope, and he had an overwhelming urge to maintain the sparkle he now saw in them. He turned back to the work console and began tapping away busily on the keyboard. The screen sparked to life.

Having returned from the broadcast suite and uploaded the footage, DV-8 and 10-CC stood at the large window running the length of her office looking out across the city. The brilliant white of many of the party buildings had faded somewhat to an ashen grey, resulting from a mix of arson and poor maintenance ever since the incident. DV-8's brow furrowed as he noticed the white flag on top of the party HQ now had another flag flying just next to it: the gaudy, star-spangled monstrosity he had seen popping up more and more over the last week or so. The crowd outside the party HQ had dispersed somewhat. Still, any solace this gave him was soon washed away as the disorderly, mingling, colourfully dressed crowd had simply spread across the city. The once quiet, spotless, empty streets were filled with people ambling along to nowhere in particular. He couldn't help but pity their directionless, purposeless wandering and hoped their new plan would bring about at least the beginnings of a return to normality, direction, and purpose. He noticed a couple walking along the street in the most curious formation. Each had an arm stretched out and their hands clasped together with interlocking fingers as they meandered lazily along.

He couldn't help but notice that he and 10-CC were standing close enough that their hands could reach out and touch in the same fashion. Of course, they didn't, and why would they? From their window, high up in the broadcast department building, they could see countless infoscreens dotted around the city. They shifted nervously, eager to see them light up and fill the city with the Supreme Leader's wisdom once again.

"Do you think this will work, brother?" She asked with a shaky, faltering voice.

"I hope so, sister."

Together, they waited.

Across the city, BB-01 shared the same view from the window of his office high up in what he now referred to as 'The Former Party HQ' building.

"I'll be right with you," he called behind him in a shaky voice. He also shared the same feeling of anxiety with his former comrades.

The plush office was filled mainly by a long, wooden table in the centre. On one side sat a row of people in the black uniforms of the former security officers. On the other side sat a row of people in the curious, dull green uniforms, the sleeves emblazoned with the red, white and blue flag. These were now erver present across the city.

"So, how'd you like the movie?" the General boomed, sat in the middle of the row. "One of our classics. They don't make 'em like that anymore!"

Thank God, BB-01 thought. He grimaced and rubbed his temples, returning to his position in the centre of the opposite row, facing the General.

"If we could get back to the matter at hand," a woman in a black uniform blurted out with barely concealed frustration.

"Sorry!" The General laughed with exaggerated contrition. "You know, you're supposed to be less authoritarian now, sweetheart! Did you forget to send her the memo?"

The General laughed heartily again as he reached across the desk and punched BB-01 on the arm playfully. He did not reciprocate in kind and managed only a polite smile in response.

"We must do something about the resistors," she continued to protest.

"Resistors?" BB-01 inquired.

"There are reports from several quarters of people still going to work, carrying out their patrols, attending party meetings, even wearing the uniforms, that sort of thing."

"Resistors, they're calling them," a corporal offered from the end of the long table.

"Freaks, more like it!" The General barked with another hearty chuckle.

"This does indicate a worrying amount of support still exists for The Party, for the Supreme Leader," she continued, despite the General's interjection.

The General leaned back in his chair and waved his hand dismissively.

"Well, I say we just tell 'em the truth."

"No!" BB-01 blurted out in panic.

The tense silence that followed his outburst was broken by the fanfare ringing out across the city. BB-01 couldn't help but let out an instinctive sigh of relief at the familiar and now surprisingly comforting sound.

"Wait," he frowned, his instinctive relief dissipating into a more logical concern, "did we do that?"

"I don't believe so, sir," the female officer replied.

BB-01 sprang up and rushed to the window just in time to see the infoscreens illuminate the city.

Strolling hand in hand along the street, Jane and John had no idea that DV-8 was watching them from high up in the Broadcast Department building. They swigged casually from brown bottles filled with a strange drink the new soldiers had introduced them to at the party HQ party. They couldn't recall the name, but they didn't care as one of the side effects of the drink was a carefree attitude.

They were joining a crowd of people taking part in one of the seemingly never-ending street parties that had started after the incident, when a deafening sound stunned the crowd into silence. Many had just about managed to forget the noise of the fanfare, and the sudden remembrance shocked them to the core. The crowd turned as one, the most regimented movement they had made for some time. John wrapped a reassuring arm around Jane's shoulders. They looked up to the huge infoscreen mounted to the motorway overpass above them along with the rest of the crowd, just in time to see it light up.

The living room of a small apartment on the outskirts of the city now looked drab with ashen grey walls and a thin carpeting of dirt, grime and discarded brown bottles. The apartments in every Party building were usually cleaned daily, but all maintenance teams had abandoned their posts since the incident.

The old fanfare rang out from the large infoscreen on the back wall, and the door to the sleeping quarters burst open. AC-DC rushed out, trying his best to pull on his old white overalls as he rushed to the centre of the room. The discarded bottles clanked together and scattered across the floor as he crashed to the ground in his frantic haste. He quickly scrambled to his feet, zipped up his overalls and stood to attention in the centre of the room. He crossed his arms across his face and could only hope the Supreme Leader would forgive his transgressions as he struggled to see through watery eyes. He wiped the budding tears away and looked up to see his infoscreen light up, just as they were all over the city.

DV-8 felt 10-CC's gaze lingering on him as they waited. After thirty seconds, he became alarmed. This was highly unorthodox. What possible reason could she have for staring at him? How could she not be glued to the infoscreen on the building opposite when they were about to see the Supreme Leader make an address for the first time in over a week? Yet the stare lingered. DV started to think that maybe she was not quite the party member he thought she was – perhaps she had succumbed to deviance like all the others. He was about to turn to confront her when she broke the unbearable silence.

"Huh? Wasn't your hair parted on the other side yesterday, Brother?"

He cursed himself silently.

"Er, yes. Well, you see…"

At that moment, the once familiar fanfare rang out across the city, and thousands of infoscreens lit up simultaneously. They both turned to watch and took a deep breath in perfect unison.

- X -

THE WEEKLY REPORT ENDED, and the Supreme Leader's face filled the screens:

> *My friends, I am greatly troubled by the reports I have received from home, but we always knew that the end of the war on deviance would be a struggle.*

10-CC watched intently from the window of her office but as the Supreme Leader's voice rang out from the infoscreens she became distracted. She noticed that DV-8 was silently, almost imperceptibly mouthing along to the words of the Supreme Leader. She couldn't help an admiring smile as the message continued:

> *For those who still believe, for those who still wish to see an end of deviance, know I have not forsaken you. For those still willing to fight, we will be amassing outside of the party headquarters tomorrow at half past twenty-four or 'noon' for those who prefer classic time, and we will send a message that this deviance will not stand!*

The Supreme Leader crossed his arms across his face and nodded briskly, performing the party salute. DV-8 and 10-CC reciprocated in kind. The Fanfare blared out across the city once again before the screens faded to black. They both took a deep, contented breath, puffed out their chests triumphantly and faced one another. The same disturbing sensation he had felt the day before came over DV-8: What to say now? He had been enlivened by concocting their plan together and enjoyed carrying out the tasks they had set themselves, but it was now complete, and he had no idea what else to talk about. He found himself staring blankly back at her and felt as if the silence in the room was somehow getting louder. He concluded that the best thing to do was leave immediately without another word and attend to his nightly patrol as usual. He gave her a curt nod, then spun sharply on his heel and headed for the exit.

"Er, brother?"

He swung back around quickly to face her.

"Yes, sister?"

"I imagine you've been struggling to carry out your nightly patrols alone, what with such a dramatic rise in infractions lately."

"Indeed, sister."

"Maybe I could accompany you this evening?"

10-CC shifted uncomfortably and was fidgeting with her hands. *It must be contagious*, he thought. There was no other reason for such odd behaviour.

"As a way to say thank you for your help today?"

The pleading in her eyes had returned. DV-8 felt powerless to say no. He only hoped she would not be too much of a distraction from his patrol duties.

The nightly patrol was anything but routine, which was typical of the nightly patrols since the incident, so it actually was quite routine, in a way. They weren't even halfway through the patrol and had recorded over 100 incidents of deviance between them. Additionally, they'd reported dozens of infractions by other party members, including an infraction each against one another. DV-8 had recorded the fact that 10-CC suggested joining him on his nightly patrol, which was highly unorthodox, and she had recorded the fact that he had allowed her to join him on his nightly patrol, which was equally unusual. Interestingly, neither recorded that the other was confirmed as a deviant. DV-8 had the nagging tendency to give the benefit of the doubt, and if 10-CC was honest, she secretly enjoyed the company during such troubling times.

They had almost completed their patrol route and were coming up to DV-8's apartment building when they spotted a small group of security officers wearing black uniforms at the end of the street. He stopped, remembering how he had seen the security officers outside the theatre accosting the man in party uniform.

"Look Brother! I haven't seen a security patrol team around here since the incident!"

This was true, he thought to himself. Such a sight should be cause for celebration, and the fact they were not accompanied by any of the strange soldiers in the dull green uniforms made him even more hopeful.

"They must have seen our message and decided to take up their patrol routes again. It's working, brother!"

10-CC's eyes lit up with excitement, and her mouth opened with wonder; an expression she hoped would soon be rightfully outlawed once again but for the time being, she couldn't suppress it, try as she might.

He couldn't quite share her excitement but was tentatively hopeful as they continued along the street towards the five security officers. The small group huddled together, discussing something of seemingly high importance. Perhaps 10-CC was right, he thought. His mind began to spin – maybe their plan did work, maybe this was the start of the return to normality they had been hoping for; perhaps the patrol team were rounding up everyone who had succumbed to deviance ever since the incident, everyone who had failed the test. His pace quickened, buoyed by her optimism. DV-8 was keen to share with the security officers their reports and accusations to help with their investigations.

As they approached, the group leader spotted DV-8 and 10-CC.

"THERE HE IS!" he yelled, pointing down the street toward them.

Confused, they stopped and looked back down the street searching for the deviant the officer must have been pointing at.

It was empty.

DV-8 looked into the face of the man pointing in their direction; he was just too far away to make out clearly, but DV-8 could have sworn he recognised him from somewhere.

"YOU TWO! Don't move!" he barked again.

It dawned on DV-8 that they were pointing at him. He turned to 10-CC, a look of terror in his eyes, and without a word, she understood. The group advanced towards them. They both spun on their heels and began walking in the opposite direction, trying to look inconspicuous and failing miserably.

"Stop!" the security officers called out, charging along the street.

DV-8 looked over his shoulder. The head officer closed in, his face now in full view. It was UB-40, the owner of the secret book, the man he had reported and sent for re-education. He had heard excellent things about the re-education team and their work; even so, he was doubtful they could so quickly drive the deviance out of the mind of a man who subscribed to such ridiculous and sacrilegious notions as he had read in that book.

DV-8 and 10-CC broke into a sprint.

Thankfully, even though the state-sanctioned daily exercise classes had not been taking place since the incident, they had both continued performing the exercise routines independently and remained at the peak of Party mandated fitness. The security officers had not kept up with their exercise regimens and had spent several days attending the spontaneous street parties that had popped up all over the city. They gave chase as best they could, but quite some distance quickly extended between them and their prey. They watched breathlessly as their targets rounded the corner at the end of the long street and laboured along after them.

DV-8 and 10-CC screeched to a halt at the edge of the pavement. The pedestrian crossing sign flashed red. He glanced frenziedly up and down the street. There was no traffic, which was lucky. Since the incident people ignored the curfew and used the roads at all hours of the night. They could hear the rhythmic, metallic thud of the officers' iron-heeled boots striking the pavement as they closed in. DV-8's stare remained fixed on the flashing red sign, imploring it to change and allow them safe passage.

It stayed red.

Taunting them.

"Forgive me, sister."

"Whatever for, brother?"

DV-8 grabbed her by the arm and raced across the street, dragging her along with him. The security officers rounded the corner just in time to see their quarry reach the other side and hurried along in pursuit. The pedestrian signal changed and flashed green. Despite this, a row of cars came speeding down the road, one after the other, blocking their path. The security officers faltered and stepped back onto the pavement, stranded on the opposite side of the road to their targets.

"Hey! Are you blind?" UB-40 cried in vain at the passing motorists as he pointed to the green crossing signal. "It's like no one follows the rules anymore!"

DV-8 and 10-CC disappeared around another corner and stopped, searching frantically for a way to lose the pursuing gang.

"Dave!"

They looked at each other confused by the curious, exotic sound they had heard carried on the wind.

"DAVE!" The sound rang out again, and DV-8 tried to remember where he had heard it before.

"V-D EIGHT or whatever it was!"

They looked around to see Jane standing in the doorway of a nearby apartment building, leaning against the door frame, smoking a cigarette, and smiling back at them.

"Everything OK?" she asked casually, blowing plumes of acrid smoke into the air.

They huddled inside the small foyer of Jane's apartment building. DV-8 hunched forward; hands clasped to his knees as he tried to catch his breath. Jane peered out of the small window on the front door to the building and watched the security officers go charging past along the street in pursuit of the two fugitives.

"So, the reporter has become the reportee!" Jane laughed as she swigged the last remnants from one of the brown bottles DV-8 had seen so many of his former party members enjoying since the incident. She tossed it casually on the ground. 10-CC winced at Jane's carelessness, adding to the trash and detritus that already covered the floor. 10-CC itched to take out her electronic notebook and start recording all the very evident infractions, but she was also grateful for Jane's help.

"Thank you, sister."

"Jane's the name," she replied with a smiling but stern rebuttal of the language of The Party, "and what do I call you?"

"My serial number is..."

"For fuck's sake, not you as well, love!"

They gasped at the sound of the curse word but quickly tried to suppress their shock. This wasn't easy, as such language used to be punishable by imprisonment; it was quite rare these days to hear an outlawed word such as 'love'.

10-CC recoiled as Jane leered towards her, but the confined space meant there was no escape from Jane's searching finger. It crawled, spider-like, over the serial number printed on her chest. She felt powerless.

"Let's see, C-C, C-C...CiCi!" Jane exclaimed, causing 10-CC to flinch and bump up once again against the foyer wall.

"Pardon me, sister?"

"Cici! That's a nice name for you!"

"Oh, well, er..." 10-CC struggled for the right words. She could feel her notebook, sat in the front pocket of her overalls, burning a hole in her chest. She longed to start scribbling away in it, but all she could do was let out a stifled cough as Jane blew another cloud of acrid smoke from her cigarette, filling the cramped space. DV-8 stood up straight, having finally caught his breath, only to swallow a lung full of smoke.

"Thank you, sister," he spluttered.

Jane gave him the same cautionary glance she had given 10-CC at the word 'sister'. He returned a slight, apologetic smile.

"But I'm a little surprised. I have to ask, why did you help us?"

"Ah, I dunno. Just felt like. You see, I can do whatever I feel like. Isn't that great?"

DV-8 and 10-CC glanced at each other, confused and unsure of the point Jane was trying to make.

"Anyway, come on up," Jane shrugged, "won't be safe for you out there for a while."

She squeezed between them in the small passageway: feeling their rigid posture, an almost unbearable tension in their bodies as they both itched to reach for their notebooks. She smiled politely and led them towards the staircase at the back of the foyer.

DV-8 and 10-CC's eyes met. They were bulging with panic. This came as some relief to them both; at least the other also recognised the seriousness of the situation. It was forbidden for Party members to enter any living quarters to which they were not assigned, but at the same time, they knew that Jane was right; they couldn't go back out yet; the security officers would be searching the streets for some time.

"Let's go!" Jane called, holding the door open.

They nodded at one another in a show of silent understanding. For the moment, they must side with the lesser of two evils. This was a phrase they were both familiar with from their history studies at school. 'The lesser of two evils' was the slogan used by The Party during their first successful election campaign. It was just after the first world war in 2509 during which, unfortunately, many archives of historical records and documents were lost or destroyed. As it turned out, they never needed to come up with another campaign slogan since, in all but one subsequent election, the Supreme Leader had run unopposed. It came as a shock to voters that year when a particularly ambitious senior leader decided to throw his hat into the ring. Sadly, the pressures of running a political campaign must have gotten to him. Just before the election, he committed suicide by shooting himself in the back of the head six times, then injecting himself with a lethal dose of poison before throwing himself off the *Supreme Leader's First Dog* memorial bridge.

Some people just aren't cut out for politics.

They filed along behind Jane up the stairs in silence with their heads bowed, looking like they'd been caught and were on the way to prison rather than being saved as they had been. For now, at least.

"They were snooping around earlier today asking questions about you, Dave."

"Oh?" he replied. Eager to find out more information he forgot to challenge her use of the strange sound she insisted on using when addressing him as 'Dave', rather than his serial number.

10-CC looked to him, silently indignant at his response to the clearly deviant moniker. He hung his head again.

"Yeah, don't worry though. I didn't tell them anything. None of my business, after all."

"Thank you. Although I believe technically it is deviance to knowingly mislead a security officer."

Jane stared back at him with astonishment. She was ready to admonish him for his lack of gratitude for her help and even his own lack of self-preservation, but his blank, earnest expression rendered her speechless.

"It's just…I wouldn't want you getting in any more trouble, sister, when the Supreme Leader returns. Not on my account."

She couldn't find any words capable of breaking through his cordial smile.

"Thanks," was all she was able to manage.

"Quite alright, sister."

She opened a door leading to a long corridor of apartments, gestured for them to follow, and tossed her exhausted cigarette onto the floor as she reached the front door of her apartment. She stood before it expectantly. Nothing happened; the automatic door did not slide open as expected.

"You see," 10-CC began, "with the maintenance teams gone you can't even open your…"

Jane pounded on the door with her fist. Her guests flinched.

"Hey, open up! it's me!"

DV-8 and 10-CC shifted uncomfortably, trying to find space on the floor with their feet that wasn't already taken up by discarded food containers, cigarette butts, or empty brown glass bottles. The door slid open, and John's smiling face appeared.

"Visitors!" Jane exclaimed, slipping past him and into the apartment.

John poked his head out into the corridor and spotted the two fugitives staring back at him.

"Dave!"

Instinctively they both went to perform the party salute but thought better of it, given the situation. They stiffened their spines, straining every sinew in their bodies to keep their arms from crossing over their faces. Instead, they did their best to reciprocate in kind, forcing stiff, unconvincing smiles back at him.

- XI -

GIVEN THAT THE APARTMENT was structurally identical to his own, it was surprising how alien the whole environment appeared to DV-8. The white walls had yellowed from constant cigarette smoke. The usually spacious, open-plan living room felt cluttered and claustrophobic, it was filled with soft furnishings and even softer lighting. This was a stark contrast to the usual harsh but clear lighting from the single fluorescent strip-light in the centre of the ceiling that was once powered by the national grid, but which no longer appeared to be working. Time was, of course, that the district lighting was powered by the Supreme Leader's preferred method, gas. However, this was expensive and temperamental. It became clear that gaslighting the entire population was too tall an order even for the SL himself, try as he might. But most egregiously of all, the infoscreen on the back wall of the apartment was covered by a colourful, patterned sheet that some very careless person had strung across it.

There were strict guidelines on how Party members' quarters should be maintained and how individual rooms should be decorated. There really was no excuse for breaking these rules, especially as The Party offered mandatory Feng Shui classes which taught Party members exactly how each and every room should be laid out:

- o Firstly, all rooms should be painted white and white only.
- o Second, all rooms should contain only essential furniture.
- o Thirdly and most importantly of all, the number one rule was that all rooms should have an infoscreen that is unobstructed and in full view, at all times.

To cover up the screen, particularly with such garish material, was unacceptable. *I mean, that's obvious. That's just Rooms 101,* DV-8 thought. Ever since the incident, he had longed to look to the infoscreens for instruction and guidance as he had done all his life and this bright, tacky material blocking the screen felt like a further insult from the deviants who had taken over. He noted that the sheet didn't quite cover the infoscreen's camera lens. He was convinced that these must still be being monitored as part of the Supreme Leader's test and knew that he must do everything he could to differentiate himself from the deviants currently occupying the apartment.

"Come on in, man!" John declared, slapping DV-8 on the back, and encouraging him inside.

DV-8 flinched. He tentatively stepped forward and immediately drew back as he saw someone or something occupying an offensively plush sofa. On closer inspection he saw there were two people who almost looked like one; intertwined, contorted in an unorthodox position, and laid across the sofa in a confusing tangle of flesh. He could only assume that the curious item of furniture was responsible for their physiological collapse as it appeared to offer very little in the way of postural support. Unlike the regulation orthopaedic chairs which helped Party members maintain perfect posture which had seemingly been thrown away by these ungrateful new residents. It was a man and a woman. Their fingers and limbs were interlocked, and their arms wrapped around one another. DV-8 was beginning to wonder if they had been in some terrible accident when the man uncoupled himself. He hurriedly sat up at the sight of the two fugitives.

"Who the f…"

DV-8 and 10-CC stood to attention in the centre of the room and, in unison, crossed their arms in front of their faces and nodded curtly, performing the party salute. No one reciprocated, in kind or otherwise.

"Brother, sister. Please forgive our intrusion," offered DV-8 by way of introduction.

He was greeted with a menacing silence.

"They're in a bit of trouble," Jane explained, collapsing down on the opposite sofa, "I said they could hide out here for a while."

The man stood and approached. He came close to DV-8 and looked him up and down, examining him the way he might examine an alien if he ever came across one. DV-8 glanced nervously around the room trying to avoid his probing gaze.

"What do we call them?"

"My serial number is…" DV-8 began, but he was quickly cut off by a cry of protest from Jane.

"Hey! No serial numbers in this house. His name's Dave."

DV-8 cleared his throat, shifted uncomfortably, and shot Jane a disapproving look.

"My house, my rules!"

"Sorry, man, she can be a bit of a tyrant," John said, placing a reassuring but unwelcome hand on the backs of the two fugitives, "guess that won't be a problem for the two of you though, hey?"

John chuckled as the fugitives exchanged a confused glance before he slumped down on the sofa beside Jane. *What was this expression he kept using*, DV-8 thought, referring to him as 'man'? Was this some sort of deviant version of the party-sanctioned 'brother' that they were now supposed to refer to each other as? Along with the already confusing sounds they seemed to have taken as names instead of serial numbers, he didn't relish learning even more strange and confusing deviant dialect. Still, they would have to tolerate it for the time being if they wanted to remain hidden from the security patrol. The man finished examining 10-CC in the same impersonal manner he had examined DV-8 before resuming his position of entanglement with the woman on the sofa.

DV-8 and 10-CC could not take it any longer. They quickly snatched the electronic notebooks from their top pockets and began urgently scribbling away.

"What are they doing?" the woman asked.

"Reporting us." Jane shrugged.

"Yeah, for when the Supreme Leader returns!" John exclaimed with exaggerated importance and a scathingly sarcastic tone.

DV-8 turned to the enmeshed couple.

"Your serial numbers, please?" he asked politely.

"We don't do that number shit anymore," the man snarled back, "we're our own unique people now, with our own unique names!"

DV-8 looked up expectantly from his notebook, pen poised.

"My name's John," the man answered proudly.

DV-8 looked from this new John to the original John, unsure how to proceed. Jane and original John offered no help, looking away as if this was an argument they didn't want to be dragged into again.

"What? It's a cool name. There can't be two Johns?" New John protested.

"No, it's fine," DV tapped the pen against his notebook, "it's just now I'm not sure what to put down because I've already got…"

"Just put 'John 2' or something," he snapped, cutting DV off.

"Oh...so you do still use numbers, brother?"

"Are we going to have a problem here?" John 2 asked as he started to untangle himself from his partner and stand up again.

"No, no. It's fine." DV protested and quickly scribbled down 'John 2' in the DEVIANTS column.

"And you, sister?" 10-CC asked John 2's partner as she pulled him back onto the sofa.

"My name is..."

She then proceeded to clap twice, gave a short, sharp whistle and followed that up by emitting a low hum that lasted around 10 or 15 seconds. Once it became clear this was all she was going to offer by way of a name, DV-8 and 10-CC looked at each other, again unsure how to proceed, before hastily scribbling down in their notebooks:

John 3

DV-8 couldn't help but feel John 2 staring a hole through him. He looked up from his notebook and was met by a menacing glare.

"Forgive us, brother, but when the Supreme Leader returns..."

"So, I suppose you'll be at the party HQ tomorrow with all the other freaks?" John 2 interrupted.

"Yeah, can you believe that video they put out yesterday?" John 3 asked no one in particular, as she lit her cigarette. DV-8 and 10-CC shared a quick, concerned glance, both realising they had become 'they.' Jane noticed their postures stiffen and their sharp intake of breath.

"Oh well, it's a free country last time I checked," Jane replied, struggling to get up from the cushiony sofa, so used to the rigid orthopaedic chairs as she was. She stood still for a moment and considered her own words carefully, "Although, not the time before that, to be fair."

Jane skipped across the room with her usual carefree buoyancy and reached out to take 10-CC's hand. She recoiled sharply and looked back at her, horrified.

"Sorry, I just wanted to show you your room for the night."

"The night?" DV-8 cut in.

"Of course. You aren't thinking of going back to your apartment tonight, are you?" Jane protested, "don't you think they'll be looking for you there?"

"She's right, man, you should listen," John called over from the sofa as he swigged from his glass bottle.

"Oh, I suppose…"

"Great, OK, let me show you," Jane said, leading 10-CC through a door to an adjoining bedroom on the right side of the living room. DV-8 caught a flash of the pleading eyes he hoped never to see again as she was led away, they disappeared into the other room. He felt powerless to help. John

3 sprang up and followed them into the bedroom. DV-8 had no idea what to do, so he did nothing. He stood to attention in the centre of the room, looking up at the camera above the infoscreen with his own pleading eyes.

The bedroom also shared the same dimensions as the ones designated to all party members but was again an alien, unfamiliar sight for 10-CC. A mattress lay on the floor, much wider than her own or indeed any she had ever seen. It looked almost as if it could accommodate two party members, but for what reason such a mattress would be designed, she could not conceive of. It was mystifying. In the corner of the room stood a piece of furniture that looked vaguely like the steel wardrobes Party members were provided with to store their overalls. But this one was different. It was constructed from brown wood and had curious, ornate carvings at its edges.

"You know, it's no wonder they caught up with you so quickly," Jane said, looking her up and down, "walking around dressed like that."

"Yeah, only resistors are still wearing the uniform," John 3 added.

"Resistors, sisters?" 10-CC rhymed, unintentionally of course – wordplay being a long since outlawed act of deviance after all.

"Well, that's the technical term. Most people are just calling them freaks."

10-CC looked back at them with genuine confusion, and they smiled at each other.

"You know, you lot," Jane explained, then she stood up on her tiptoes, exaggeratedly stiffened her posture, puffed out her chest, crossed her arms and bowed in a parody of the party salute. 10-CC instinctively, and earnestly reciprocated in kind but was met with laughter by the other two.

"Anyway, if you don't want to get caught," John 3 called back as she made her way over to the wardrobe in the corner, "you'd better change."

John 3 swung back the wardrobe doors. Instead of revealing Party overalls, it was stuffed with unusual garments – all manner of colours and styles.

"They've been handing out some great stuff ever since the takeover," John 3 said as she began leafing through the poorly organised clothes spilling out onto the floor.

"Let's see if we can't help you fit in."

Jane wrapped her arm around 10-CC's shoulders. 10-CC resisted her immediate urge to wriggle free and tried her best, in vain, to relax and smile convincingly back at them.

DV-8 stood resolutely in the centre of the living room, trying to ignore the menacing, penetrating gaze from John 2, which had not relented for a moment.

"You sure you don't want to sit down, man?" John asked, barely bothering to look up from the strange, glossy book he was reading. It consisted primarily of pictures of female party members without their party overalls for some reason.

Before DV-8 could answer, John 2 sprang up quickly from the sofa and brushed angrily past him.

"Where are you going?" John asked, still not sufficiently interested to lift his eyes from his weird picture book.

"Out."

"Where?"

"Just out. It's a free country, remember?"

John shrugged and continued reading as John 2 made his way out of the door, which he would have slammed if it was not a sliding door. He glanced derisively in DV-8's direction as he left, who did his best to remain still and stoic in the centre of the room, highlighting his detachment from the others for the benefit of the camera lens above the infos-creen.

"Hot in here." John groaned as he heaved himself up from the sofa. "Mind if I turn the heat down?"

John made his way across the room to the thermostat on the wall. DV-8 froze, not because of the temperature (he actually was a little too hot, if anything), but in shock, as this was something he had never been asked or needed to consider before. The Party had always regulated and mandated the temperatures of all Party buildings, and while he had seen the thermostat on the wall of his apartment before, it had never occurred to him to use it. The Party had conducted extensive research to find the optimal temperature and controlled the heating systems to ensure this was consistent across all offices and dwellings. They had discovered that a slightly colder temperature was best. It encouraged party members to work harder to keep warm and helped to marginally increase productivity. This is why all party buildings had been kept at a bracing 45.1 Fahrenheit for as long as DV-8 could remember. He looked up to see that all the time he had been turning this over in his mind, John had been standing at the thermostat, looking back at him expectantly. John watched as DV-8 shifted uncomfortably at the thought of making his own decision.

"Hey man, it's hardly a life or death…"

"I am not a 'man'. I am a number!" DV-8 exploded, surprising even himself, "I am D-V Eight!"

His words died out, and he found the room now engulfed in one of the strange, uncomfortable silences he was becoming all too familiar with. John stood still, his hands raised in protest, backed up against the wall. He tried to look as unthreatening as possible and deter any further outburst from his houseguest.

"Dave! Come in here!" Jane yelled from the other room.

So great was DV-8's relief to be called away from the unpleasant atmosphere he had unwittingly created that he waived the usual indignation he felt against being referred to by the odd name they had bestowed upon him. He moved quickly and obediently into the bedroom, leaving John in the awkward vacuum that had filled the apartment since his outburst. Slipping past John as he went only served to amplify the awkwardness, but he was pleased that the camera

170

lens above the infoscreen would have recorded his outcry. Anyone watching would be in no doubt of his continued resolve and commitment to the ways of The Party and the Supreme Leader.

No sooner had he entered the bedroom before he was shocked into a stunned silence of his own by a sight that had him yearning for the uncomfortable tension of the living room.

"What do you think?" Jane asked as she stepped aside and gestured to 10-CC.

Instead of her usual white overalls, 10-CC was wearing a dress of striking red. It took him a moment to take in the vision before him. Her bare legs immediately caught his eye as the dress didn't quite reach the floor. Her milky white skin contrasted sharply with the scarlet silk in a not-unpleasant fashion. The material was softer than the party-approved polyester overalls and it allowed the shape of her thighs and the contour of her hips to subtly reveal themselves. The soft light from the small lamp in the corner of the room also proved to be much more forgiving than the usual strip lights. The dim light was so warm it appeared to radiate from within her. It gently illuminated her skin and allowed shadows to accentuate any curves visible, thanks to the dress's plunging neckline.

Despite the obviously deviant nature of such a garment, DV-8 was surprised to find that he was not immediately repelled by the vision standing before him. He would have almost had to admit, if only privately to himself, that this look improved on her usual white, rigid uniform. That is, if not for what he saw when his gaze finally reached her face. He saw in her eyes a deep panic. Intense desperation. A return of the pleading helplessness he had tried so hard to subdue ever since he had first witnessed it that day on the train platform. That gaze which reminded him so much of the eyes of his co-habitant, DV-9 and of the secret book owner, UB-40, as they were being led away by the security officers at his behest. That gaze that he hoped, once again, he would be seeing for the last time.

"I was just saying, you two are bound to get caught running around in those old uniforms, so we thought…"

DV-8 cut Jane off, turning to her sharply and decisively.

"We appreciate your help, sister." He spoke in a calm yet authoritative tone that he had not heard passing from his own lips before, born out of necessity to help his comrade. "But as you know, we remain loyal to the Supreme Leader and will not denounce him in this fashion."

Another uncomfortable silence filled the room as his words died away, but this time his conviction was enough to stop him from caring or even noticing.

"Isn't that right, sister?"

10-CC looked up and was heartened by his strong, benevolent expression that almost put her in mind of the Supreme Leader himself.

"That's right, brother."

"Fine, fine!" Jane threw up her hands. "We were only trying to help."

She handed the white overalls back to 10-CC, took John 3 by the hand and led her out of the room.

"I suppose we'll just leave you both to it."

Jane pointed out the double mattress on the floor to John 3 as they left the bedroom giggling conspiratorially. The reason for this was completely lost on the two fugitives, and indeed, DV-8 and 10-CC barely noticed it as they smiled slightly at each other.

"Thank you, brother."

"Of course, sister."

Her coy smile soon curled into her more usual anxious grimace as she held up the white overalls she clutched in her hands and cleared her throat.

"Oh, er…of course, sister"

DV-8 instinctively span around and was immediately met by the bedroom's back wall, inches away from his face. He dared not readjust his stance or step back but stood perfectly still to allow her to change into her familiar, uncomfortable, and yet somehow much more comfortable white overalls.

Downstairs, John 2 stood leaning against the frame of the front door to the apartment building. He took a final drag of his cigarette and blew a plume of smoke up into the cold night air. He was about to return upstairs when he noticed the security patrol rounding the corner onto the street, still hunting down the two fugitives.

DV-8 and 10-CC lay on their backs on the odd, oversized mattress, as far apart from one another as they could possibly be without falling off the side and onto the cold, concrete floor. From above, their rigid posture gave the impression of two soldiers standing perfectly to attention. It was as if they were stood in line waiting for the regular weekly update to begin as they both sorely wished they would be again some-day soon. Their proximity put DV-8 in mind of when they stood looking through the window of the Broadcast Department offices together triumphantly watching their illegal broadcast play out on the infoscreens. Curiously, just as he had then, he couldn't help but note that they were situated close enough that their hands could reach out and touch one another's. He was doing his best to drive this irrelevant but persistent observation from his mind when she suddenly broke the silence.

"Well, goodnight, brother."

"Indeed, sister."

Somehow, no sooner had he uttered the words than an-other heavy, awkward silence engulfed the room. If only he could identify the cause of this perplexing phenomenon, he would be able to prevent them from continuously occurring. Instead, he recalled there was something he had wanted to ask 10-CC and was relieved to be able to fill the silence, if not deter it completely.

"Actually, sister."

"Yes?" She replied urgently, indeed even slightly before he had finished speaking.

"There was something I wanted to ask you to do for me."

"Yes, brother?" she replied, this time much less urgently and with far more hesitation.

"It's something I have never asked anyone to do for me before, but I feel I must."

This time she waited a long time before replying, as long as she realistically could, hoping that something, anything, would interrupt them.

"Yes, brother?"

For some unknown reason, she too suddenly became aware of their close proximity.

"I'd like you to report me, sister."

The sigh of relief that passed her lips was sucked back in sharply as she realised the seriousness of his request and her surprising reluctance to carry it out.

"Whatever for, brother?"

"For crossing the street against the signal during the chase. It was clearly red."

"Oh, yes, I suppose it was."

"I'd hate for the Supreme Leader to think I was trying to hide anything from him upon his return." He explained, staring up at the ceiling, making sure to move only his mouth as he spoke and nothing else for fear they might come into contact with one another.

"Well, I suppose you had better report me to then, brother," she replied, just as stoically, "I crossed too."

"Yes, sister, but only at my behest," he protested.

"Still, better to be safe than sorry. I'm sure you'll agree."

"Indeed, sister."

As carefully and precisely as they could, they both reached into the top pockets of their overalls and pulled out their electronic notebooks. They were careful not to disturb the surface of the mattress, lest it yield and draw them closer toward one another. The infractions were hastily recorded, and the notebooks returned to their top pockets.

"Well, goodnight, sister."

"Indeed, brother."

This time the silence that followed was not heavy with tension but light with a satisfying resolution, that small piece of party business having been dealt with efficiently. They each couldn't help a slight, content curling upward at the corner of their mouths as they closed their eyes and eagerly anticipated the mourning and the response to their illegal broadcast with a renewed sense of hope for the future.

They were shaken from their visions of a return to party rule, the glorious resurrection of the Supreme Leader and a restoration of normality by a deafening banging sound from the living room.

"Hey!"

They heard Jane call out in protest before she was quickly drowned out by more loud banging. They sat bolt upright, robotically. They became self-consciously, painfully aware of their closeness, and a crushing sense of guilt and shame rushed through them. The door to the bedroom flew open, and the five security officers in black uniforms burst in. The two fugitives leapt quickly to their feet and flung themselves apart from one another.

"We weren't…"

DV-8's protest was cut short, and his words reduced to an unintelligible groan as all the air was driven out of him by a strategically placed baton belonging to one of the security officers. He collapsed to the floor, which made him wish he was still on the strange, oversized mattress despite the abstract tension he had felt between himself and 10-CC. The impact of his body hitting the cold, unmoving concrete was somehow much less abstract.

"GET THEM READY."

He heard the command barked in a familiar voice – the owner of the secret book. It was the unmistakable sound of UB-40.

DV-8 felt his arms wrenched behind his back and his hands clasped together just before another blow to his side expelled all the air he had managed to recapture into his lungs. He heard the continuing protestations from Jane and John coming from the living room and then heard them quickly silenced. In a flash, 10-CC was lying next to him again, only this time not as rigidly and stoically as before. She was now loose, limp even, and her body sprawled out across the hard concrete. DV-8 looked to her face, dreading that the desperation and pleading had returned to her eyes but needing to see it all the same; he was saved from the troubling sight as her eyes were closed, but this came with its own set of concerns. He was soon relieved of these worries when a final blow to the back of his head forced his own eyes to close and plunged him into complete darkness and all-pervading silence. At least this silence was not awkward, as he was not conscious of it or indeed anything else from that point on. While being unconscious was obviously not ideal, it did mean he would be unable to commit any more infractions than he already had during what was, it had to be said, rather an eventful day for DV-8. For that, he could be thankful at least, or rather he would have had the intervention of the security officers not rendered that or any other thoughts impossible for the time being.

Jane and John huddled closely together as they watched the security officers drag the lifeless bodies of the two fugitives out of the bedroom and across the living room. They looked on helplessly as the security officers reached the front door to the apartment. There they saw John 2 looking in with a sheepish, almost ashamed expression. The two fugitives were taken out, followed closely by UB-40. He turned to John 2 and spoke with grim satisfaction as he left.

"Thank you for your vigilance, brother."

John 2 could barely bring himself to look up at the others who stared at him in shell-shocked disbelief.

- XII -

DV-8 HAD HELD THE SAME POSITION for most of his working life, and the lack of promotion meant he worked in an office in the outer quarters. Despite going through several reallocations, he invariably ended up assigned to apartment buildings in that sector every single time too. The towering Party HQ building was an ever-present sight for him, looming far off in the distance during his working hours and nightly patrols. It acted as a beacon of hope and motivation for him to carry out his duties to the best of his ability. All senior Party members worked in the party HQ building, and most had apartments there too. He would often look up to the white flag atop the building wavering gently in the breeze and dream of one day being promoted to the Upper Party. He had previously thought he would do anything to get into the party HQ building, anything that was, but this.

He was now inside, but rather than occupying one of the plush offices or luxury apartments on the upper floors, he found himself occupying one of the holding cells on the lower floors of the building, deep underground. He had seen only darkness ever since the security officers took them but based on the endless flights of stairs he'd been dragged down, he knew where he must be. Once the metaphorical black veil of unconsciousness had lifted, he opened his eyes to see nothing but darkness still, owing to the much more literal, actual black veil placed over his head.

"What's with the hoods?"

DV-8 heard the indignant yet unmistakable voice of BB-01 coming from beyond the veil.

"And the handcuffs? Get those off, now!"

"Sorry, sir, old habits and all that." A security officer removed the veil from DV-8's face and set about unshackling his wrists.

The relief at regaining his sight was tempered by what it allowed him to see – a tiny cell of concrete walls and steel bars. UB-40 and one of the security officers who had arrested him stood just behind BB-01. He was looking down at DV-8, horrified. The only thing that could temper the tempering of his relief was that 10-CC was still next to him, sitting on the small bench attached to the cell's back wall. As their handcuffs were removed, BB-01 held his hands up in protest and tried as best he could to adopt his usual expression of unshakable affability.

"Now, listen," he began, sounding more like the accused than the accuser, "let me start by apologising. I only asked for you to be brought to see me. I didn't ask for all this."

He gestured towards the hoods and handcuffs the two officers behind him were now holding and gave them both an accusatory glance. UB-40 and the other officer shared a glancing, guilty smirk as BB-01 turned back to the prisoners.

"I know we met before, but that seems like a long time ago now. A lot of changes, a chance to start over." BB-01 spoke slowly and calmly like a trainer attempting to soothe a cornered, dangerous animal, "My new name is Brien. What about you two?"

BB-01/Brien reached out and offered a handshake to the prisoners, who immediately stood to attention, crossed their arms in front of their faces and nodded, performing the party salute while reciting their serial numbers. DV-8 held the salute firmly, and he looked into the camera above the ever-present, ever-blank infoscreen against the far wall just outside his cell. Brien did not reciprocate in kind. Although he had only recently stopped using the party salute himself, he couldn't believe how ridiculous it now looked and inwardly scoffed at their ludicrous stance. His thoughts were interrupted by one of the soldiers in the strange, dull-green uniforms who entered the room and marched straight up to BB-01.

"SIR!" he barked, before proceeding to stomp his right foot hard against the floor. He raised his right hand, open palmed to his forehead with an exacting, mechanical motion.

Brien reciprocated this much more sensible, totally dignified, and traditional salute earnestly and puffed out his chest proudly as he did so.

"Yes, private?"

"You are needed upstairs urgently, sir."

"Thank you, private."

They repeated the salute and response once more. DV-8 and 10-CC couldn't help but inwardly scoff at their ludicrous stances. Brien turned back to the prisoners, his self-serious expression morphed into placid neutrality and his voice softened to a placating tone.

"As I was saying, I hate to have to bring you in like this..." he struggled to continue, and the pitch of his voice increased in an attempt to make the accusation seem lighter than it was, "but I believe you are the ones responsible for that little broadcast yesterday? Is that right?"

The prisoners looked to each other for answers and, finding none, remained silent.

"Hey, look. I don't want to have to keep you here," Brien continued, sounding like a desperate teacher attempting to bond with a pair of unruly students, "all I want is for you both to enjoy your new freedom! Promise to do that, and we can release you!"

Another awkward silence. DV-8 found this one all the more bearable as he was fairly sure this was not one he'd created. Brien's words hung heavy in the air and seemed to echo off the bare concrete walls, further accentuating the disparity between his words and the situation they all now found themselves in.

Brien grabbed a chair, spun it around and sat down; legs splayed wide apart, elbows perched on the back rest, hands clasped together under his chin. It was a seating position DV-8 had never seen before, but one that he was immediately sure would never have passed regulation in the good old days of The Party.

"It's just," Brien continued trying his best to ignore the uncomfortable silence he had unwittingly created, "we can't have any more talk about The Party or the Supreme Leader returning or any of that business. It undermines everything we've worked for, everything we're still working for".

He looked from the face of one prisoner to the other, but their blank expressions gave him nothing. He ploughed on regardless. "So, if you'll just promise to stop it with all this…" As he searched for the next word, he realised his tone was becoming harsher and more authoritative, so he chose a distinctly diminutive expression which unfortunately only highlighted the anger in his tone by its disparity. "This…silliness. Then you're free to go! OK?"

He looked hopefully from one prisoner to the other once more but was met again with a wall of inscrutable stoicism.

Brien's head dropped in a moment of uncharacteristic open frustration, "Look, I'm needed upstairs. Just think about it, OK?"

While his previous 'OK' sounded like a question, this 'OK' sounded much more like an order. Brien hurried off, shaking his head, and disappeared from the very restricted view that the tiny dimensions and steel bars of the cell allowed.

The two security officers filed out after him. The cell door slammed shut.

"We letting them stay together?" The officer snarled.

"Yeah, shouldn't be a problem with these two freaks," UB-40 replied as they took up their positions outside the cell.

DV-8 and 10-CC returned to their bench and sat in silence. They stared at the camera above the infoscreen on the wall outside their cell, and each gave it a small nod of grim determination.

Brien marched quickly back into his large office high up in the party HQ building. The General stood facing out of the huge window overlooking the entire city, giving a panoramic view, all the way out to the perimeter wall.

"What's the prob..." Brien began, but the General span around, stamped his right foot on the ground and raised his right, open palm to his forehead, saluting him.

"Sir!"

Brien, clearly flustered at forgetting the new protocol, quickly reciprocated in kind. "What's the problem?"

"There's even more of them now, sir." The General replied with an almost accusatory glower before stepping aside and gesturing to the window.

Brien reluctantly, stepped up and looked down to the forecourt in front of the party HQ building. As soon as he saw what the General was referring to, he scrunched his eyes shut and pressed his forehead against the cold glass, searching for any sensation, however small, that might distract him from the current situation. The forecourt was filled by a large crowd of people, standing to attention in perfect rows of ten, all dressed in the white (although some were now slightly yellowing) overalls of the old Party uniform.

All eyes were trained on the huge infoscreen on the side of the party HQ building.

Waiting.

Several hundred feet underground, the two prisoners remained sitting in silence in their cramped cell. The only view available to them, the backs of their two captors standing guard: UB-40 and his fellow security officer.

"What? So they're just standing out there?" the security officer asked UB-40.

DV-8 and 10-CC listened closely.

"Yep. Just stood to attention, in their stupid white uniforms. Waiting to be told what to do. It's pathetic," he replied.

"Ha, freaks."

DV watched as the two guarding officers straightened their backs and continued standing to attention in their black uniforms.

A voice crackled through the radios strapped to their shoulders, "Code yellow. Report upstairs for new assignments right away. Over."

"YES, SIR! Right away, sir!" they barked in reply, before filing out, leaving the prisoners all alone.

The overheard conversation gave the captives a tiny inkling of hope; they looked to each other with slight, tentative smiles. The moment their eyes met, they remembered the camera above the infoscreen watching them. They snapped back to facing dead ahead, expressionless. While imprisonment was obviously not ideal, DV-8 noted that the curious tension between himself and 10-CC had somewhat dissipated. The hard surface of the small bench and concrete wall they now found themselves sitting against helped them to retain a stiff, rigid posture. It didn't amplify their physical closeness the way the soft, inviting surface of the oversized mattress had done the previous evening.

"Brother?"

"Yes, sister?"

"What are we going to do?"

He instinctively looked to the infoscreen as he had done his whole life whenever he was looking for answers. The blank screen reflected back his own image, but this did not even register with him. The disappointment of the blank screen and his yearning for the constant guidance it once provided was all that he could think about.

"I don't know," he replied.

"SIR?" The General's barked, one-syllable question reverberated around the office.

It ripped Brien from his momentary cerebral escape. He lifted his head from the glass windowpane, opened his eyes and slowly turned to face the General.

"What are we going to do?" The General not so much asked as ordered a response.

Brien couldn't help but look instinctively to the infoscreen, which still occupied the back wall of his office, so used to consulting it for guidance as he once was. His head dropped as he was reminded that they had covered up the infoscreen by draping one of the colourful, gaudy red, white and blue flags across it.

"I don't know," he replied.

- XIII -

BY THE AFTERNOON, WORD HAD spread across the city about the strange assembly forming in front of the old Party HQ building. Many former Party members had already been outraged and frightened in equal measure by the previous days broadcast. Those who believed the broadcast had come from The Party itself were terrified that it could mean a return to Party rule. Those who thought it was simply the work of the 'resistors' or 'freaks', as they were becoming colloquially known, were utterly baffled by their continued support for The Party. This radical deviation from the prevailing, popular opinion that life was so much better now without The Party, or the Supreme Leader would not stand, and many former party members resolved to do something about it.

The forecourt outside the party HQ building was heaving with people. On one side stood the organised group of resistors, standing quietly awaiting the glorious return of the Supreme Leader. On the other side was a group of former Party members dressed in an assortment of different clothing and in no discernible order, a mass of humanity shifting and throbbing with violent intent. Both groups were separated by a resilient line of security officers in black uniforms doing their best to keep the screeching, braying mob of normal people from the quiet, orderly group of deranged and delusional resistors.

AC-DC, his devotion to the Supreme Leader renewed, stood stoically at the end of one of the lines nearest the mob, staring up at the blank infoscreen. John 2 sneered at him from the very front of the mob, attempting to force back the security officers.

"Freaks!" he spat over the heads of the officers at no one in particular.

From his office window, Brien continued to watch the scene unfolding below. He could feel the tension even from his vantage point on the top floor of the party HQ building. He sat back down at the long, wooden table with a row of people in black uniforms and opposite them, a row of people in dull-green uniforms. In the epicentre, sat the General.

Brien scrolled through his electronic notebook, looking for any distraction from the current situation. He barely listened as the officer sitting opposite the General finished briefing the rest of the group.

"They have been asked to disperse several times but refuse to listen to reason." she concluded.

"This will not look good", the General broke in, "the whole world is watching us right now, since the revolution.

We must show that we have the situation under control. I suggest we have my men forcibly remove them."

"Oh yeah, that will look great!" she shot back, "we did all this so nobody would be forced to do anything!"

The General clenched his fists, incensed at being interrupted.

"Then what do you suggest?"

"We've been discussing, and we could…" she broke off, wincing as if she had to force the words from her lips, "tell them the truth."

The words caused a cold sweat to break out on Brien's forehead, and he was suddenly reanimated, as if awoken from a deep sleep.

"No!"

"Don't worry, sir," the General winked at Brien with a conniving smile, "we'd protect you."

"Not an option," Brien stated with more conviction than he had been able to muster up for some time. He stood and paced the room anxiously, arms behind his back.

The General chuckled, sat back and flashed the woman a mocking smile, "Well, then."

"We did also discuss the prisoners," she interjected.

"What about them?" the General snorted.

"We just pin all the blame on them. Get them to go out there and tell everybody the broadcast was all their doing. The Supreme Leader's not coming back, The Party is done, they made it all up, and everyone should go home."

The General raised his hand and pointed a condemnatory finger in her direction but stopped short just before speaking. He tilted his head as he considered her words further. His expression softened as he experienced the unfamiliar feeling of his brow furrowing, as if in thought.

"You think they'd do it?" one of the General's soldiers asked, narrowly beating the General to the next logical question moments before it occurred to him.

The General silenced his man with a swift fist pounding on the desk, making it clear who was asking the questions.

"Well, would they?"

"Not likely," another officer responded, "we tried speaking to them. They aren't cooperating at all."

"Well, I'm sure my men could *convince* them," the General offered with another conniving smile.

"No," his adversary across the table quickly rebutted, "no 'convincing', it's not how we do things anymore."

"Well, what then?"

Brien had absent-mindedly wandered over to the bookshelf and was inspecting it, subconsciously attempting to remove himself from the situation entirely. A solitary, remaining copy of *The Book* sat on the bare shelves. Shortly after the revolution had taken hold, most copies of *The Book* had been burned. It was a protest against the outgoing administration and their draconian practices such as corporal punishment, imprisoning dissenters and book burning. But this single copy must have been overlooked. Hardly surprising,

Brien thought as he picked it up and started turning it over in his mind. The operation had not been particularly well planned, he had to concede that things were much harder to organise without force or the threat of re-education. He flicked through the book aimlessly, regarding it as one would a fossil, a relic from another time. He landed on a particular page and stopped. He looked up at the others. His clear excitement caused a silence to come over them. They looked back at him expectantly.

"Maybe there is a way we could get them to cooperate," he offered, holding up what was possibly the last remaining copy of *The Book* in existence.

The two prisoners continued sitting, staring straight ahead. The lack of work orders to think about or party business to worry over was getting to DV-8 more and more as the unfilled days rolled on. He turned the incredible situation he found himself in over and over in his mind. If only The Resistance hadn't taken over, if only the revolution had never occurred, if only they appreciated what they had before, none of this would be happening.

He thought back to the secret book he had read shortly before the takeover in search of answers. What exactly did people not like about life under the rule of The Party? What exactly were The Resistance resisting? He remembered that the confused manifesto was peppered with the 'F-word' – fascism. It repeatedly accused The Party of enforcing fascist policies and claimed the Supreme Leader was himself, a fascist. This was the point that proved to DV-8 these people were truly deranged. It was as if they wilfully misremembered that the Supreme Leader was the man who banned all mention of fascism in public life. Time was, classes in school would teach all about different instances of fascism in human history, how fascists took power, what made a populace vulnerable to fascism and the warning signs that fascistic ideas were taking route in a society. The Supreme Leader banned any such teachings and later went even further when he forbade anyone from using the word fascism in political discourse by penalty of removal from office. He decreed that accusing a fellow party member of fascism could even lead to jail time, in some cases indefinitely. But sure, the guy who hated fascism so much he removed the concept entirely from civilised society by imprisoning anyone who studied, taught about, or even mentioned the word, he's the real fascist!

Their delusional reasoning was unbelievable.

He would have loved to see The Resistance try and push some of their crazy ideology once the Supreme Leader was back in charge. The SL would wipe the floor with them in any meaningful debate; it was well-known he was the greatest political thinker of his time. It was even said he knew the secret to making communism work, but he was unwilling to share it.

DV-8 found himself looking around for something to occupy his wandering mind. He noticed through the steel bars that the other cells across from them, which at one time would have been filled with deviants eagerly awaiting their re-education treatments, were now empty. How sad, he thought, to see a once thriving industry brought to its knees.

His mind moved on, and he found himself mentally measuring the dimensions of his prison cell. He was surprised to find that they matched exactly the dimensions of his bedroom and were perhaps even a little bigger than the dimensions of the office cubicle he was required to occupy for up to ten hours every day. He couldn't help a short, sharp pang of outrage – why should deviants enjoy the same luxurious lifestyle that the Supreme Leader provides to his more committed and obedient party members? But this outrage soon passed and was replaced by the more familiar sense of admiration for the SL and his boundless benevolence, which was extended even to the most undeserving in society. His mind continued to wander, desperate for anything of substance to cling on to; this free time was starting to become a real nuisance.

Mercifully, the clang of the cell door flying open broke the long silence and focussed his mind instantly.

"You're both wanted upstairs."

DV-8 looked up to see two security officers standing at the open door, looking down on them in every sense of the word. The two prisoners stood up obediently.

"NO," the officer barked, sending them both quickly back to their seats. "One at a time, you first." The officer pointed squarely at DV-8.

He could feel 10-CC looking at him but could already sense what expression she would be wearing on her face – not one he was keen to see. He followed the officers out of the holding cell.

"There he is!"

Brien met DV-8 with open arms and a bright smile. It was as if they were old friends meeting at a party rather than a prisoner who had been marched up to the office of his captor.

"Come in, come in!"

Brien offered him a chair on the opposite side of his desk.

"How's it going?" Brien asked with feigned sincerity as DV-8 sat down.

DV-8 stared blankly back, not really understanding the question, and beginning to miss the solitude of his quiet, cramped cell over the spacious, comfortable, but much louder office.

"Anyway, I've got a bit of a problem I could use your help with," Brien began in as casual a tone as he could muster.

"Another patrol you need me to cover, brother?" DV-8 asked, in what was the closest he had ever come to making a joke in his life, although entirely unwittingly. Such was his desire for normality, in the moment, he was hopeful that this was the problem he would be asked to help with.

"No, no...not that," Brien narrowed his eyes, trying to discern how sincere the question had been, "actually, come and have a look."

Brien led him over to the window. DV-8 peered down into the courtyard of the party HQ building. Both crowds had increased in number, the resistors in their organised rows and matching uniforms and the seething mob intent on removing them. The line of security officers separating the two had also widened to keep them apart. Brien watched his face closely for a reaction, but there was nothing of note. Although DV-8 was indeed pleased to see the resistors lined up in their party uniforms, he didn't find it in the least bit surprising. Of course, they would come, he thought. Of course, they wanted a return to the old ways – who wouldn't? With no reaction to go off, Brien led DV-8 back to the table in the centre of the office.

"So, you see. Those people are all down there because of the little message you put out yesterday," Brien said, almost admiringly, "all waiting for the Supreme Leader's glorious return!"

DV-8 nodded sensibly, despite Brien's exaggerated, sarcastic tone, agreeing with everything he said.

"But the problem is those other people down there. They're also here because of your little message, except they didn't like it as much. In fact, we're starting to worry that

197

those people may hurt your people if this goes on much longer."

Brien leant forward and looked DV-8 straight in the eyes, trying to elicit a reaction stronger than polite nodding.

"And we wouldn't want that now, would we?"

This caused DV-8 to stop and pause for thought.

"No, of course not, brother. Anyone threatening violence should be detained immediately. Could I suggest re-education?"

"See, we're not as keen as the last administration on *re-education*." Brien spoke this last word slowly with an ironic, sarcastic tone which was entirely lost on DV-8. He simply assumed this was some new, hip, deviant accent that he looked forward to reporting once things went back to normal.

"No, what we'd like to happen is this," Brien continued, "you go out there and tell everyone you were the one behind the broadcast. That you made it all up, the Supreme Leader isn't coming back, and they should all just go home."

"But I didn't make it up, brother. It was simply what was to be included in the weekly report. The footage was one hundred per cent accurate."

Brien's head dropped. He looked at the copy of *The Book* now sitting on the table for a moment before reluctantly lifting his head and eyeballing DV-8.

"And what if I told you, if you don't go out there and tell them all you made it up and tell everyone to go home, something bad might happen…to you."

"That's a sacrifice I'd be willing to make, brother," DV-8 responded instantly, without hesitation.

Brien couldn't help but privately concede that some of The Party's old persuasion techniques would come in really handy at that moment. Just a few floors below them was the 'political think tank.' Political opponents would be hoisted above a 3200-gallon tank and slowly lowered into the piranha-infested water, giving them time to have a good think about any issues of contention they may have had with the government. He almost regretted having it drained and disassembled shortly after taking power, but he did have one last trick up his sleeve.

"I thought you might say that," Brien replied, "but what if I told you, if you don't do as we ask, something bad might happen…to your friend."

"Friend, brother?"

"Your friend downstairs, Ten C-C, is it?"

"Well then…" DV-8 went to answer immediately once again, but this time the words stuck in his throat. Brien's eyes flashed with triumph, and a sly smile passed his lips, confident he had finally broken through.

"Well then," DV-8 spoke slowly and with a grave tone. "That would be a great shame, brother. But I'm sure she too would want to make that sacrifice. For the greater good."

Brien's head dropped again, the most he had ever allowed it to in one day, lest the veneer of his constant affable, cheerful nature begin to crack.

"Will that be all, brother?" DV-8 asked.

As he was led away from Brien's office, he saw 10-CC being marched out of another office at the other end of the hallway. Similarly, as the officers forced him into the lift, she was forced into the lift at the other end of the hallway. They arrived back at the cell at the same time and were hurriedly shoved inside by their attendant officers. The cell door slammed behind them with a loud clang. The officers left, and they sat in silence.

"I want you to know that I stayed true, brother. I betrayed you instantly."

"Indeed, sister. And I, you."

The small, contented curl began to creep in the corners of their mouths once again as they sat staring straight ahead. DV-8 considered her words carefully, 'I want you to know'. It seemed she was concerned about the feelings of others, something traditionally discouraged by The Party, or at least one other, him. She was concerned with how he felt about her. In another moment he realised that he was concerned how she felt about him. He found this very strange as he was always taught that caring about the feelings of others was a decidedly deviant trait, one that was such a strain on the human mind it soon led to feelings, which then led to emotions and, finally, inevitably gave way to madness. Stranger

still was the realisation that it was not an altogether unpleasant sensation and didn't feel like quite the burden he was
always taught it would be.

- XIV -

THE GENERAL WATCHED THE increasingly volatile situation in the courtyard from Brien's office with a disgusted grimace. He had taken a moment to step away from Brien and his advisors, who had retaken their seats around the long wooden table.

"I really thought that would work." Brien groaned and tossed the last copy of *The Book* into his fireplace.

"They could probably tell you were bluffing," the General said. He returned to the table, startling Brien from watching the book's pages blacken and curl up at the behest of the flames engulfing them.

"Sometimes you gotta show people you're serious if you want them to cooperate."

"Yeah, but we don't actually want to hurt anybody," the woman sat across from him protested.

Her striking beauty was accentuated by the passion and fire in her eyes, lending her words a convincing air of sincerity.

"Welcome to the real world; you wanted to be a part of it, after all."

The General was grimly defiant. She had been his regular adversary ever since the revolution, as she called it or the takeover, as he did.

"Look, just let me and my men go down there, and we'll soon…"

"Let me talk to him," she cut in, causing the General's frown to harden. "The prisoner, I mean, I think he may still help us."

They looked to Brien expectantly. He startled slightly as he was reminded that he was the one making the decisions around here. He nodded, willing to try anything that would absolve him of any responsibility for the situation.

DV-8 found himself being taken from his cell, marched along seemingly endless corridors, and shoved into another room. He quickly noted this was not another plush office, in fact it was scarcely bigger than the cell he had been sitting in. The walls were bare. There were no windows and no sign of any ventilation. However, the most troubling thing by far was the distinct lack of infoscreen. He couldn't remember the last time he had been in a room without an infoscreen. Now he came to think of it, he wasn't sure he ever had been. It made him feel very uncomfortable, knowing he wasn't being watched. He glanced around nervously searching for some sort of instruction or guidance. It came in the form of a disembodied female voice coming from a speaker above.

"Take a seat."

His relief at finally having some clear instruction on what to do distracted him from the fact that he recognised the voice. He approached the small metal table and sat facing the door and another empty seat across from him. After a few moments, the woman who had asked to see the prisoner walked in. The woman who had been advising Brien ever since the takeover. The woman who originally reported DV-8 as the man behind the illegal broadcast and the woman who was once DV-8's roommate.

One might wonder how all of these women could fit through what was a relatively narrow doorway. The answer was that these women were all one and the same. They were all DV-9.

"Sister?"

He felt as if a great weight were lifted from his shoulders at the sight of his former roommate. He looked into her eyes, delighted to see that they no longer were filled with pleading desperation as they had been the night she was taken away. This initial relief soon evaporated as he noticed the anger and menace radiating from her. Worse still, it seemed to be directed toward him.

"Hello...brother."

He went to speak but found no words. He watched her in a dumb, staring silence as she calmly sat opposite him and smiled a triumphant, defiant smile.

"Did you not wonder? How they caught up with you so quickly? How they knew exactly where to find you?"

"Sister?" Repetition of the last thing he said was about all he could manage.

"Did it not occur to you to ask? No, you don't like to question things, do you?" The smile intensified. "They found you right outside your apartment building, our apartment building. I reported you. So, I suppose now we're even."

"Even, sister?"

"I'd listened to you prattling on about what was going to be in the next weekly report. The minute I saw that stupid broadcast, I knew it was you."

She looked strange to him now, dressed as she was in her black uniform. He had never seen her in anything but the white overalls of the party, but regardless of the colour, he was most thankful that there was no rip in her uniform this time. Fortunately, no errant flashes of skin were visible, and she was no longer trying to seduce anybody. His powerful yet unwitting allure had seemingly worn off – for now.

"But why have me reported?"

"Why? After what you did to me! I wanted you to feel how I felt – scared, betrayed, alone."

She peered deep into his eyes, looking for any signs of the hurt she had hoped to cause but was disappointed by the blank, expressionless eyes staring back at her.

"Did it not make you feel bad," she asked, almost pleading for a reaction, "watching them drag me away?"

The sight of the security officers taking her away flashed through his mind. He'd been trying to repress the thought of it ever since it happened. This was another point in The Resistance's secret book which he found very hard to understand; the desire for something called 'freedom of thought'. He desperately wished for some party business to occupy his mind, some mindless instruction to follow, a report to prepare; anything other than this 'freedom of thought' which allowed any thoughts, even unwanted ones, to drift into one's mind without warning. If anything, he wished his thoughts were more constrained so he could never play out her arrest in his mind again. He glanced around nervously at the wall where the infoscreen could usually be found.

"Looking for something?" she snarled through gritted teeth, remembering what happened the last time they were alone in a room together.

He looked back, wanting to offer something in reply. Nothing came.

"Sorry! No infoscreen here. Nothing to give you the answer. Nothing to tell you what to say or to think or to feel. I want your answer. Did you feel bad?"

"I was concerned for you, sister," he managed to force out quietly, "you needed help."

"Help? Do you know what would have happened to me if The Resistance didn't save me? If the takeover had been even a day later? I was scheduled to be…"

"You would have been helped, sister. You would have been happy."

She was dumbstruck. Not so much by the ridiculousness of his words but by the complete sincerity with which he spoke them. Her expression softened as the anger and malice which contorted her features seemed almost ludicrous in response to the innocent, earnest sympathy etched on the face looking back at her.

"You really believe that don't you?"

It was now her turn to feel uncomfortable and longing for any distraction from the conversation at hand. She paced back and forth across the room.

"They need your help, you know? They need you to take the blame for all this Supreme Leader returning nonsense, The Resistors, and all the trouble they're causing. They're up there now trying to think of ways to break you, get you to cooperate, to give up on whatever stupid mission you think you're on. Trying to work out what you care about, what you're afraid of."

He watched her cross the room. Her movements became more decisive and her tone became harsher in an attempt to recapture that earlier air of triumph.

"So, I told them, it's this!"

She turned to him, opened her arms, and gestured around the room at nothing in particular. "This is what you're afraid of. You've got no Party business to discuss, no

207

reports to deliver, no infoscreen to tell you what to do. There's just you."

She leant forward, placing her open palms down on the table. Conversely, DV-8's hands curled up into tight fists as she moved her face close to his. He felt her breath on his cheek.

'Then again, there is something else, isn't there? Something you're even more afraid of."

She sat back and smirked knowingly across at him but was shocked to be confronted once again by an entirely blank expression.

"What's that, sister?"

"You know. Everyone knows."

She looked to him for some recognition but soon let out a groan, exasperated that her words were not inducing the effect in him she hoped they would.

"You do know," she reiterated, less sure that he did know with every passing moment, "don't you?"

"Sister?"

"For God's sake!" She threw her up her hands. DV-8 wondered why she was referring to the Supreme Leader by his old moniker. No one had called him 'God' for years.

"Fine. I'll go and get him."

"Get who, sister?"

"Him. The Supreme Leader, of course."

She stood and abruptly left the room, leaving DV-8 to ponder her parting words echoing around his mind. Was she really going to get the Supreme Leader? Was he really here? How could that be?

His mind raced. He found himself once again lamenting the idea of 'freedom of thought', and his bafflement that anyone would wish for it was stronger than ever. If the Supreme Leader was here, does that mean they had taken him prisoner, too? He found this hard to believe as the SL was famed for his prowess in hand-to-hand combat. He had represented The Party every four years for the last three decades in Judo at the Olympics and, according to the news reports, had won more consecutive gold medals than anyone else in the competition's history. It was a shame DV-8 had never had the chance to see the Supreme Leader compete in person, but unfortunately, they had never been chosen to host the Olympics. The International Olympic Committee had cited a whole host of human rights violations as the reason they could never host the games, but DV-8 knew these claims could not be true. After all, FIFA had no such qualms with awarding them the World Cup, and in fact, they now hosted the international soccer tournament most years.

He decided there was no way they could have captured the Supreme Leader. This is a martial arts expert we were talking about, after all. Not only an expert but an innovator, the man who single-handedly invented the 'double karate chop', which, while invented single-handedly, required both hands to perform correctly, as you can imagine.

But if he hadn't been captured, how was it he was here?

DV-8's mind continued to wander, and his spirits lifted as another possibility entered his mind. Maybe the test was over. Maybe his refusal to give in to Brien's demands was the final trial, and the Supreme Leader would soon be here to inform him that he had passed the test, set everything back the way it should be and possibly even promote him to an Upper Party position. Yes, that must be it, he thought to himself. It must be since the only other explanation was that the Supreme Leader was cooperating with The Resistance, which would mean...

As the freedom of his own thoughts was becoming too much to bear, DV-9 returned and mercifully gave DV-8 something else to focus on.

He instinctively straightened his back and sat up in his chair. He started desperately fidgeting, brushing down his uniform and combing back his hair as if there was anything he could do that would be worthy of meeting the Supreme Leader himself.

DV-9 watched him with something approaching pity.

"Proceed!" She called back into the corridor, then stepped aside and stood to attention against the wall opposite him.

The door burst open, and a squad of security officers filed in. They inspected every inch of the room, and as there weren't all that many inches, it became rather crowded in a hurry. They checked under the table and the chair. They ran their hands along every inch of the wall and floor while intermittently barking into the radio mics strapped to their shoulders, "CLEAR!"

One of the officers dragged DV-8 to his feet, spun him around and pressed his face against the back wall. DV-9 couldn't help a slight wince as she watched the security officer drive his elbow into the back of DV-8's neck while he frisked him.

"ALL CLEAR!"

DV-8 was shoved back down into his chair. The security officers lined up against the wall next to DV-9 and waited. He was shaken up, but his eyes remained intently fixed on the door. After a few breathless moments, it creaked open, and Brien reluctantly shuffled in with a sheepish, apologetic grin.

He slowly sat down opposite DV-8.

"Hi."

DV-8 craned his neck to look past him.

"Forgive me, brother. I don't have time to talk any more. The Supreme Leader is expected imminently."

Brien glanced nervously from DV-8 to DV-9 and then sat up, attempting to catch DV-8's eye, which remained fixed single-mindedly on the door.

"He'll be able to solve your problem as well, brother," DV-8 continued without looking at him, "once he arrives."

"Well, I'll do my best." Brien fixed his face with the friendliest smile he could manage as DV-8 finally looked down from the door and caught his eye.

"Sister?" He looked to DV-9, confused.

"You wanted him, well...here he is." This curt response was all she offered in explanation, pointing at Brien.

"Well, not exactly, but I'm the closest you're going to get these days. If it's any consolation, I never met him either, and he was my great-grandfather!"

"Grandfather, brother?" he asked and quickly looked to her again for answers, "Sister?"

"Just listen," she instructed, almost sympathetically.

"See, they kept his death a secret so as not to cause any panic. They carried on using his image but really, behind the scenes, my grandfather became the leader. Then my father after him. It was the easiest way."

DV-8 had to steady himself, which he found odd as he was not moving an inch. The whiteness of his knuckles also struck him as odd as they gripped the table in front of him – hard.

"Then, when my father died," Brien continued, "it was my turn. I was still just a kid, but they told me I had to preserve the legacy, told me I had no choice. They ran everything really, The Party elders, not me."

He half turned to DV-9 and the line of Resistance soldiers as he spoke, exuding an air closer to that of a prisoner under interrogation rather than any kind of leader, Supreme or otherwise.

"They just gave me little jobs to do. I was mainly in charge of keeping track of everyone's social credit score and maintaining the league tables, ranking everyone in the right order; making sure the deviants were punished and the most loyal followers were rewarded. If you really think about it, I'm hardly even to blame. I mean, I was only ordering followers."

He was met by blank stares from his men, who stood over him and looked down at him more like a jury of his peers than loyal subjects.

"I tried, I really tried," he continued, turning back to DV-8, "but I just couldn't keep it up any longer. You have no idea how hard it is to be forced to live a life you never chose, never wanted. To have every aspect of your life controlled every minute of every day. It was hell."

DV-8 was having such a hard time even processing what was being said, he didn't notice DV-9's eyebrows almost hitting the ceiling in response to Brien's statement.

"Anyway, I decided I couldn't take it anymore, so I cut a deal with the U.S, The Resistance too. I helped plan the takeover and took a job in your department for a while so no one would suspect me once it was done. Then when the time was right...well, you know the rest." Brien leant forward and looked into his eyes, but what he was hoping to see was unclear; understanding, compassion, forgiveness? Either way, DV-8 was in no state to offer any of these and was still attempting to process Brien's words.

"See, that's why we need your help." DV-9 stepped forward and stood next to Brien. "We need all this talk of the

Supreme Leader to stop. We need the resistors to go home. Suppose they discover that their precious Supreme Leader is dead, and the real Supreme Leader is the head of The Resistance. Who knows how they'll react? Not to mention how everyone else might react if they find out their great liberator, their new hero, was their oppressor all along."

"So, what do you say," Brien cut in, "now you know the truth, that he's not coming back. How about you go out there and tell everyone the broadcast was all you, you made it up, a stupid prank, and everyone needs to give up and go home?"

"I don't believe you." DV-8 managed to squeak out.

"Oh, come on! There was an entire revolution in one afternoon! Didn't you think that was strange? I let it happen!"

"It's true, everything he said," DV-9 offered. She was more sympathetic than Brien, who was tired of the conversation and becoming irritated, so unaccustomed was he with having to ask people to do his bidding rather than simply telling them.

"I don't believe you," was still all DV-8 could manage.

"Fine," Brien pinched the bridge of his nose and sighed, "I think it's time we showed him."

DV-8 began nervously speculating on what they were planning to show him. A room with no infoscreen was a terrifying enough sight. What next? A blank piece of paper and a pen to express all of his 'thoughts' instead of a nice, neat work order form with its reassuring, restrictive lines and boxes. More of this torturous 'free speech'? Endless babbling without purpose or direction, possibly with even more people? Perhaps even one of these terrible mass gatherings he'd heard about where people were encouraged to express themselves in whatever way they wanted – a party? Surely, they wouldn't be that cruel. He did not enjoy this new sensation of speculation. Undoubtedly, it was a symptom of this infernal 'freedom of thought', a concept that had been unfairly thrust upon him and which he was becoming less and less keen on by the minute.

Outside, Jane fought her way through the ever-increasing, ever-angrier mob. She shoved, scratched, clawed, and elbowed until finally, she pushed through to the front of the crowd. The wall of soldiers in black uniform stood unbroken before her. They obscured the view of the resistors who stood, silent and statuesque, just beyond them. She looked around at the twisted, snarling faces, gnashed teeth, and grabbing limbs that made up the crowd. She wondered what had happened to the party atmosphere she had been a part of in the same spot just a day earlier. She looked on, dismayed at the imposing wall of black uniforms, watching over them, a sight she never thought she'd see again.

A man shoved past her from behind, broke free from the mob and managed to slip between the soldiers. He marched purposefully up to the resistor on the end of the nearest line of ten, which just so happened to be AC-DC. Jane watched closely and realised the man was John 2. He lunged forward aggressively, getting right in the resistor's face. He gesticulated wildly and gnashed his teeth angrily at the man standing before him, still quietly staring up at the infoscreen, waiting.

"What's wrong with you?" John 2, whose face was contorted and twisted with rage, his teeth bared, asked AC-DC, who stood calmly and smiled pleasantly back at him, "you freaks, think you're better than the rest of us, 'ey? Is that it?"

John 2 shoved him lightly but was surprised that the push sent the man staggering backwards. He soon realised this was because he had been dragged back by Jane, who was now standing in his place. Before he could properly place where he knew the face from, Jane's fist intervened and collided hard with his jaw. John 2 staggered backwards, whereupon one of the security officers grabbed hold of him and shoved him back into the braying mob. He was quickly swallowed up by the mass of humanity and disappeared from Jane and AC-DC's view.

"Thank you, sister."

He smiled at Jane as he stepped forward and took up his place back at the end of the line again. Jane reciprocated in kind.

"You're welcome, brother."

- XV -

ALTHOUGH COOPERATION WITH the general and the U.S. military had been successful and they had been integral in bringing about the revolution, Brien had always had some sense of apprehension working so closely with them. The U.S, or to give them the full name which they adopted ever since the right-wing took over absolutely, The United Sovereign States of Republicans (they wanted a name which better reflected their commitment to small government and encapsulated their complete devotion to capitalist ideology and had been known as the U.S.S.R ever since) were the only foreign power The Party had dealt with in a very long time.

The Party had never had any meaningful partnership with other foreign governments in Brien's lifetime or for decades before that. The only such instance in fact occurred very early in The Party's existence before they adopted a wholly isolationist approach; back when almost all other nations and world leaders refused to accept the legitimacy of The Party or even recognise them as a sovereign power. All other nations that was, except for Brazil and their leader at the time, President Gilliam. The Brazilian premier was a great admirer and good friend of the original Supreme Leader, even going so far as to sponsor The Party's inclusion in the United Nations, bringing some much-needed legitimacy to their reign. Although this "special relationship" had long since disintegrated, the partnership was integral in the early days of the party's rule. Brien even remembered reading in a history book at school:

> *Though this author may be loath to admit it, and though I wish I were able to claim all successes as our own, I must admit a huge debt is owed to President Gilliam and the nation of Brazil. Our entire society, way of life, and indeed this very book you are reading right now would not exist without Gilliam's Brazil.*

Owing to the significance of this bygone association between the two countries, a curious tradition persisted ever since. Once a year, on the date of the *Carnaval do Brasil,* the infoscreens would play nothing but Samba music, uninterrupted for twenty-four hours. Senior Leaders wore ornate, feathered headdresses while carrying out their usual Party business, and Party members were encouraged to perform the Lambada whenever travelling, rather than walking, for the whole day. Mercifully, one of Brien's first orders when The Resistance took over, was to abolish this national holiday.

Had Brien not been busy dealing with DV-8, his apprehension would have certainly been made worse by the General's actions. The rest of the world had been following the revolution closely ever since it began. News that the last authoritarian dictatorship still in existence had been toppled was met with cheers and celebration. However, rumours of the resistors' protest were spreading and planting seeds of doubt about the new regime and the legitimacy of this so-called revolution. Someone had to step up to address these concerns, and in Brien's absence, the General had followed his natural proclivity for taking over.

The General stood behind a podium, bracketed by two U.S flags on either side of him, in front of the infoscreen in Brien's office. He had taken it upon himself to address the growing rumours and speak to the world's press about the resistors' protest. The infoscreen showed him a small room with a gaggle of eager reporters, scribbling earnestly away in their notepads and listening intently. They gathered around the small screen that was broadcasting the General.

"The crowd is much smaller than the reports would have you believe," he explained, raising his hands in protest, "it's one of the smallest crowds you've ever seen. Tiny. It's so small like you wouldn't believe – you'd need a microscope to see it! Really, you've never seen a crowd so small!"

One of the reporters raised her hand. "What do you say to those who have claimed you are purposefully deflating the number of people in the crowd to better reflect on how you're ruling and how popular your revolution is with the people?"

"Completely untrue."

A ripple of confused, unconvinced mumbling passed through the reporters.

"However, I would like to make it clear that this new regime welcomes any form of peaceful protest. We do not subscribe to the previous regime's dictatorial methods, and we understand the importance of being able to question authority." He finished speaking and several hands shot up among the small crowd of reporters. "I'm afraid we won't be taking any further questions at this time."

With the press conference abruptly over, the door to Brien's office burst open, and the General marched out. He accosted the first soldier unlucky enough to be passing by, a soldier dressed in the dull green uniform with the American flag emblazoned on the sleeve. The General placed a firm hand on his chest, stopping him in his tracks.

"Sir!" The soldier, although startled, moved to salute his General.

"Yeah, whatever," the General began with a dismissive wave of his hand, "assemble a squad to be deployed down in the courtyard. These resistors need to be dealt with."

"Yes, sir!" The soldier went to move but was halted by an even firmer hand on his chest.

"And keep this in-house. Only our men, none of Brien's lot. Got it?"

"Sir?"

"What? You got a question?" The General's tone made it clear that this was less a solicitation for genuine questions and more a warning against them.

"No sir, very good."

The soldier raced off along the corridor. The General returned to Brien's office, which was becoming more and more Brien's office in name only by the minute.

DV-8 had dreaded whatever it was DV-9 was going to show him in the time it took to travel down in the lift. Deep down to what felt like the centre of the earth, much lower even than the holding cell he had been held in. He couldn't imagine anything worse than what she and Brien had already revealed to him, but when they finally arrived at their destination, he realised there was something worse.

Much worse.

He was a full foot and a half shorter than he appeared in the weekly reports. His hair, which had always appeared thick and lustrous, was thinning, and the pink of his scalp bled through it. The formerly chiselled features were barely detectable under the sagging, pale skin which hung lifelessly from his face. Despite these many differences, DV-8 somehow knew beyond doubt who the man was. No matter how much he wished it was not true, he could not deny that the man lying in the glass coffin in the middle of this dark, cavernous room was the Supreme Leader himself.

Although perhaps even this was not true, the body of the Supreme Leader was clearly lying in the glass coffin, but the man himself seemed to have departed a long time ago. It was almost unbelievable to see his face so lifeless, a face which he previously had always seen looking so alive, so animated in the weekly reports. Admittedly it was DV-8 himself who usually did the animating, but still. DV-8 stood rooted to the spot as the dreaded freedom of thought he had been suffering from overwhelmed him. It conjured up so many questions, ramifications and horrors that his mind could not hold them all at once and seemed to burst, leaving only empty space behind. This nothingness filled his mind, washed over him, and even seemed to spread out from within. The cavernous room felt like it expanded even further out all around him in an instant. The darkness spread out over the whole building, over the city, beyond the perimeter wall, over everything, turning it to nothing. He stood, silent and solitary at the centre of what remained – nothing. How could anything remain as it was, now that he had seen what he saw. The lifeless body was a haunting testament to that which he otherwise would never have believed:

The Supreme Leader was *dead*.
The Supreme Leader had been *dead* for quite some time.
The Supreme Leader was *never* coming back.

He felt alone at the centre of a never-ending nothingness and couldn't feel the soft, almost sympathetic hand of DV-9 as it landed on his shoulder.

"So, there he is." She moved up alongside DV-8 slowly, watching him carefully, the way one might approach a cornered animal, terrified of how they might react.

She could tell from his empty expression that he was barely registering her presence, let alone feeling her touch or hearing her words. The room was empty and in complete darkness save for a solid beam of light shining down from high above, illuminating the glass coffin and its gruesome contents.

"They say it happened more than a hundred years ago. The Party just kept using his image in the reports and bulletins. It kept people happy, made them feel safe."

So many things suddenly made sense to him; terrible, horrible sense. He thought back on his memory of the only time he had seen the Supreme Leader in the flesh. It was always hazy in his mind's eye as if viewed through a flickering television screen. He now realised that's because it *was* viewed on a television screen. He could remember now, standing in the living room of his former plebeian family home watching the parade on TV. It was as if the astonishing revelation had unlocked the rest of his memory.

He recalled looking from the screen and beaming up at his mother, who curiously did not share in his delight at the sight of the Supreme Leader. He now realised why the panic and desperation in the eyes of DV-9 had bothered him so much because he had seen it before, for the very first time on that day, in his mother's eyes. Another question which had always niggled away, in the back of his mind, was the fact that if the Supreme Leader were alive and had been as long as The Party claimed he had been, he would be at least two hundred and fifty years old. DV-8 had always just put this down to the SL's superior genetics and famously immaculate diet, but he realised now what a fool he had been.

DV-8 looked back down at the coffin, appearing unperturbed by the sight, but this was simply a symptom of the fact that he had almost completely disassociated from his body and allowed the expanding nothingness to take him.

He was brought back to reality by a curious sight. The beam of light and the shiny glass surface of the coffin conspired to reflect his own face back at him, superimposed over the face of the Supreme Leader lying beneath the reflection. Before he could catch his own eye, he turned away quickly and took a few bold steps into the nothingness. The futility of this action struck him hard, indeed, the futility of any action from now on, based on what he had seen, and he slowed to a stop. DV-9 continued to watch him closely.

"Well, now you know. Now it's time to tell everyone else to give up and go home."

"I'd like to go back to my cell now." DV-8 spoke with a strange calm and assuredness that he wouldn't have thought himself able to achieve under the circumstances.

"Don't you realise what this means?" DV-9 moved in front of him in a defiant attempt to bring him back into his body, to force him to deal with the current situation. "Aren't you angry? Angry that they lied to you for so long. Don't you want to punish him? Don't you want to destroy his memory? Don't you want all those resistors out there to feel the same pain you're feeling?"

She held him by the shoulders and attempted to lift his head and move into his field of vision. She felt that his body was responding to her movements out of instinct and that there was no driving presence inside. His eyes appeared to be painted on, nothing more than colourful surface decorations rather than a window into anything deeper.

"You know what else this means?" Exasperated, she pressed her body against his, attempting to elicit some form of reaction or recognition. "There's nothing stopping you now. All those rules, all the fear, it meant nothing. Nothing is stopping you."

She pushed deeper into him and attempted to wrap his arms around herself. They fell around her waist but felt heavy and lifeless, giving in to her cajoling rather than making any purposeful movement of their own. She brushed her face against his.

"I could show you how much fun deviance can be."

She pressed her lips against his and was surprised to find he did not tense up or gasp, or immediately push her away. For a moment, she was hopeful that her seduction was

225

working, that he was ready to embrace deviance. This hope was instantly dispelled when she saw the blank, expressionless look of a man whose malleability was born out of total and complete apathy rather than any form of desire. She stepped back quickly, ready to scold him, but the arched anger of her features softened into a sort of wonder. A sympathetic bewilderment. She saw in him a helplessness and sorrow that was so complete, so profound that it caused her to entirely forget the circumstances that had led to it or the ludicrous, delusional thoughts which had caused it. If only for a moment, she could not recall who was right or wrong, which side either of them was on, what he had done to her in the past or the chronic delusion which must have caused him to be so shocked by her revelation. All of this was superseded by the overwhelming desire to see the hurt relieved and the life restored to the eyes of a fellow human being.

"I'm sorry...brother."

"I'd like to go back to my cell," he muttered, his voice as lifeless as the body laid out in the glass coffin beside them.

The cell door swung open with a bang. 10-CC was momentarily taken aback but relieved to see DV-8 return. Her relief quickly transformed into concern as he trudged into the cell and collapsed down on the bench beside her. The door slammed shut, leaving them both in silence. She sat staring straight ahead, trying not to be concerned, but his slumped, deflated posture stood out in stark contrast to his usual, rigid and attentive posture.

"Brother?"

He continued to sit, staring at the floor, defeated. She had never seen him like this. He slumped back against the cell wall and allowed his head to drop forward until his face almost sank into his chest, his slack features hanging from his face lifelessly. The contrast to her own straight back, stiff neck and even stiffer upper lip highlighted the difference between them. Although they sat mere inches apart, it seemed to forge a huge space between them. She stared straight ahead, trying to make sense of it, but for the life of her, she could not fathom what could have caused such a change in her fellow prisoner.

Brien had reconvened his team around the large wooden table in his office. No one spoke, preoccupied as they were with pretending to ignore the aggression growing in the unruly mob amassed down in the courtyard. The sound was mingled with warnings from The Resistance soldiers as they struggled to hold the mob back. These served to heighten the eerie silence coming from the crowd of resistors, the cause of all the trouble.

"So, you showed him then?" The General broke the silence by firing his question across the desk at DV-9.

"Yep," she replied.

"So? Is he willing to help us now?"

"Nope."

"And did you try and…you know…" Brien looked her up and down suggestively, "like we said."

"Yep."

"And?"

"Nothing."

"What, really? Again?"

"Ha!" The General half-heartedly concealed an amused snort. "That can't feel good."

DV-9 scowled across the desk but he seemed unaffected and looked right back at her with a derisive smirk.

"So, back to plan A, right?" The General turned to Brien. "Let me and my men go down there, sort this whole thing out in no time."

"Ok." Brien answered in a low, almost inaudible voice.

"What?" DV-9 protested.

Brien continued looking at the General and made sure not to turn and meet DV-9's eyes. "Ok, General. You have my permission."

"Supreme Leadership, sir!" The General went to stand, but DV-9 stood to meet him and slammed her hands down on the wooden desk.

"You know what he means by 'sort this out', don't you?"

"No!" Brien's voice rose to a shout as he finally met her damning gaze, "No, I don't. And I don't want to know. I just want it dealt with."

She was paralysed with indignation.

"Yes, sir!" The General straightened his posture and raised his hand to his head in salute. He stood and waited until Brien reciprocated in kind, even if it was slow and unconvincing.

The General marched out of the office with renewed purpose. The door slammed shut, ushering in a crushing silence. DV-9 continued staring at Brien. Her outrage soon morphed into disgust.

Brien continued to look anywhere but back at DV-9.

- XVI -

TRAPPED IN HIS SMALL, windowless cell, freedom of thought quickly led to something even worse – feelings. Although DV-8 was sat perfectly still, it felt like he was still wandering through the never-ending expanse of nothingness that had engulfed him ever since he stared into the Supreme Leader's lifeless face. Attempting to grab on to something, anything of meaning, blindly groping for thoughts, he found himself dwelling on DV-9's words; that he should be angry, that he should feel betrayed, that he should feel vengeful. He tried to latch onto these passing thoughts to anchor his mind, but he was not accustomed to handling such a range of emotions. As soon as he experienced one, he felt overwhelmed, cast it aside and continued wandering through the darkness.

He tried to reach more familiar territory by thinking logically. At one time 'logically' was his preferred and indeed only way of thinking, but it seemed even this had betrayed him now. No favourable, logical conclusions were available to him that could explain away what he had seen inside that glass coffin. Logically, if the Supreme Leader is dead, this whole thing hasn't been a test after all, and things can never go back to how they were. Logically, that meant Brien and DV-9 had been telling the truth all along. If DV-9 was telling the truth now, logically, that meant she might also have been telling the truth about what happened to party members who were reported. This means anyone DV-8 had reported in the past would be...

He strained to slow down his rushing thoughts as they became almost too much to bear. He tried to focus on an entirely different subject to stem the cognitive onslaught. He thought back to school and started silently reciting the simple maths problems he remembered learning. At least numbers were concrete, universal truths, something no one could dispute and that he could attempt to latch on to and find a more secure mental footing:

$$2 + 2 = 5$$
$$2 + 3 = 6$$
$$2 + 4 = 7$$

and so on...

He tried to fixate on the numbers and nothing else, to recite the simple equations until his brain was so full that he would forget everything else. But it was no use. He marvelled at how anyone could want or enjoy this' freedom of thought'. Wild, unfocused, purposeless, free thought that seemed to take on a mind of its own and was almost impossible to control. It brought to mind an old rumour, which he remembered would circulate around the district intermittently every couple of years or so of so-called 'concentration camps'. These rumours about huge, mysterious complexes out in the countryside would usually come from the more deviantly inclined of his comrades. Indeed, many who spoke of them were often soon reported and taken away for re-education, so DV-8 didn't give the rumours much thought. What would even be the purpose of a 'concentration camp', he would often think to himself, but now he understood all too well. They must have been for Party members suffering the ill effects of freedom of thought, who were having trouble focusing their minds and needed a little help with their concentration. He chastised himself for disregarding these rumours and taking for granted the services The Party were good enough to provide to struggling Party members. If only he could go back and sign up for one of these concentration camps, he would be first in line.

It was hopeless. No matter what he did, he couldn't stop the racing thoughts and subsequent troubling emotions. The desperate eyes of his mother on the day of the parade were a particularly persistent memory. Not long after this, The Party, on behalf of the Supreme Leader, had come to rescue him, to take him away from such a troubling sight. But who would save him now? Now he *knew* the truth about the Supreme Leader?

In complete desperation and with nowhere to turn, he instinctively looked towards the infoscreen outside his cell.

He was just about to curse himself for still looking to it for answers even though he knew no answers were coming, when something strange happened.

He did find an answer in the infoscreen. A reflection bounced off its shiny blank surface and stared back at him – not his reflection but that of 10-CC. 10-CC, who he had completely forgotten existed, along with everyone else in the world but who sat mere inches away from him staring dead ahead. The panic and desperation had returned to her eyes and was now more palpable than ever. For a moment, all his thoughts and all of his emotions, the anger, the outrage, the betrayal, crystallised and came together with a single focus.

The nothingness started to recede as a purpose for all these unwanted thoughts and emotions began to materialise. He followed this thread, and it led him out of the darkness back into the light of reality. The world came back into focus, and he could see his surroundings clearly for the first time since his gruesome discovery. It suddenly became apparent to him that the only purpose of such awful thoughts and feelings must be to stop them from ever happening to anyone else, to stop the same thing from happening to 10-CC.

"You know, sister, it's not too late."

She startled at the sudden break in the silence and his improved, energised posture.

"Brother?"

"You could do what they asked, save yourself. Apologise, promise not to do it again. Learn to enjoy your freedom."

"But brother! When the Supreme Leader returns, all will be well. You mustn't lose hope now!"

DV-8 looked deep into her eyes, hoping against hope to see that she didn't really believe what she was saying, that she wasn't really hoping for something he now knew would never come to pass. He saw a profound and deep sincerity in her eyes, an iron-clad belief that the Supreme Leader would return and make everything right again.

"Quite right, sister, quite right," He turned away from her and stared dead ahead at nothing in particular, "Just testing you, that's all."

"Oh. Well, I commend your suspicious nature, Brother. But I couldn't let you face all this alone. No…what you do, I do."

They sat for a few moments in a curiously unawkward, comfortable silence.

"Guard!" DV-8 leapt from the bench and poked his head through the bars, "tell Brien I'm ready to help. I know what to do."

The enormous stone doors to the party HQ building opened, and the General marched out onto the front steps. He cast his eye quickly over the whole scene; the resistors in their white overalls still stood steadfast and silent in their precise rows, the mob aggressively taunting and jeering at them, swelling with ever more violent intent. The line of Resistance soldiers in their black uniforms keeping the two crowds apart but being inched further back by the minute. He strode to the edge of the steps and scowled down at the people below, regardless of what faction they were in. He was followed by a long double line of U.S. soldiers clad in dull-green uniforms and carrying heavy-looking firearms. The General smiled as the soldiers passed him and made their way down the steps. The procession split into two lines, snaking around the crowd of resistors. Cheers began to ring out from the braying mob as they watched the soldiers surround the rows of resistors, who were still looking up expectantly at the infoscreen. The U.S soldiers pivoted to face inward, aiming their guns at the ever-faithful Party members. A brooding quiet descended and the mob settled. Some were relieved that action was finally being taken to deal with the resistors, while the reality of what may be about to happen dawned on others, and they were silenced by a grim foreboding. Many of the resistors glanced around nervously; some started breathing more heavily, others nervously tapped their feet. But all of them, to a man, remained rooted to the spot, standing to attention, firm in their belief that the Supreme Leader would soon return and wouldn't allow any harm to come to them. They looked up at the infoscreen and waited.

John 2 jostled for a good view from within the mob and, upon seeing the U.S. soldiers pumped his fist in the air and cheered. This quickly reminded him of the punch he had received earlier from Jane as pain shot through his jaw. Jane peered over the shoulder of a Resistance soldier from her position right at the front of the mob. Her blood ran cold as the U.S. troops took aim at the resistors. She tried to fight her way past the Resistance soldiers but was soon restrained. She caught the eye of AC-DC. He was shaking with terror but remained rooted to the spot, paralyzed by fear as much as by commitment to any cause.

The General watched triumphantly from his position on the steps of the party HQ building, and a satisfied grin creased the corners of his mouth.

Brien led DV-8 to a small room along the corridor from his office. He opened the door to reveal a small cubicle occupied only by a workstation and chair. It was almost identical to DV-8's old workstation in the News Department. Brien stood back and gestured for DV-8 to go in.

"You sure this will work?"

"Yes," DV-8 replied instantly.

"OK, I'll leave you to it. But I have to ask, what made you decide to help us?"

"Well, we're all in this together, brother."

DV-8's earnest smile was met by a blank, bewildered stare. Brien closed the door behind him, leaving DV-8 alone. He sat down at the workstation. With nothing on the screen and only his reflection staring back at him, he instinctively looked down, absentmindedly and unconsciously searching for a distraction. Luckily, he found something. He noticed that the rip in the leg of his overalls had torn open once again in all the commotion, although not entirely. Half of the tightly pinched stitching remained intact, but about a quarter inch of the rip had opened, revealing the slightest hint of the skin underneath. He stared at it curiously for a few moments.

At last, he raised his head. He saw his reflection staring back and looked him dead in the eye.

He *knew* what to do.

The screen lit up as his hands worked away at the keyboard. His reflection faded, but not before he caught a glimpse of the slight smile forming in the corners of his mouth.

"General!" The radio mic attached to the General's uniform buzzed, and a voice crackled out.

The General groaned as his attention was taken away from the task at hand and the tense scene playing out in front of him.

"General, we've received orders to hold your fire and pull your men back. Do you copy?"

"And what if I don't?"

"This is a direct order from Commander Brien. A direct order, do you copy?"

"Hey, it's a free country, isn't it?"

The General clicked a switch, and his radio mic cut out with a hiss. The strange quiet once again washed over the gathered crowds, and he enjoyed the feeling of power that came with all eyes turning to him in anticipation of what he would do next.

DV-8 couldn't help but smile to himself as he pushed the door to the cell open. He realised they had never actually been locked in, so confident were their captors that they wouldn't attempt to escape. The creak of the cell door startled 10-CC, who was falling asleep. She sprung up from the bench, crossed her arms across her face with tight fists and nodded, performing the party salute. She frowned with concern upon noticing that he didn't reciprocate in kind. He stepped back and opened the cell door wider.

"Let's go."

"We can go? How? Why?"

"Come on, I'll explain on the way out."

He quickly marched across the lobby towards the exit as she followed behind, struggling to keep up in every sense of the word.

"But brother, why have they let us go? I thought they would only let us go if we…"

He forged ahead, refusing to slow down or even turn to face her. She stopped abruptly, and her voice rose to the highest volume she had ever allowed it to before.

"Brother?"

Her voice echoing around the huge lobby of the party HQ building stopped him in his tracks.

"Please, we have to go. Please just…"

He stepped forward and reached out to take her by the hand. 10-CC recoiled and took a step back at such a blatant show of deviance.

"Brother!" she shrieked in horror.

He lifted his head and was just about able to look her in the eyes. She saw a guilty, sombre expression plastered across his face, and in that instant, she realised why they had been allowed to leave. She was sure he had betrayed the Supreme Leader and given up on their cause. She'd never felt more alone. 10-CC took a few more tentative steps back as she began to feel the same dark nothingness he had felt earlier engulf her, casting a shadow of hopelessness over everything. DV-8 stepped forward and reached out to her again, but this somehow only forged a greater distance between them.

She was overcome with the sudden urge to flee, to outrun the nothingness spreading out all around her. All she wanted at that moment was to be away from DV-8, from everyone, from the suffocating swamp of darkness she was quickly sinking into. She spun on her heel and raced across the lobby.

"Wait!"

DV-8 broke into a sprint and chased after her. Ahead of him 10-CC flung open the nearest door and raced up the staircase behind it.

The General raised a megaphone to his lips and broke the eery silence that had fallen over the two crowds; the crowd of resistors waiting for the Supreme Leader's return and the gathered mob waiting for something else, something that many were now realising they didn't want to see at all.

"Your attention, please." He directed his words towards the resistors still stood stoically in their organised rows of ten. "This is your final warning. We will be forced to take action if you do not break up this unsanctioned assembly immediately."

10-CC's mind ran without direction, purpose or hope, and so did her body. She had run up countless flights of stairs, away from the reality she didn't want to acknowledge and away from the ever-expanding nothingness that had pursued her every step of the way, just as DV-8 had. She finally came to the top of the staircase and had no choice but to burst through the door she found at the end of it if she wanted to keep going, and she definitely did. She ran out onto the roof of the party HQ building and charged across it as DV-8 emerged from the door behind her.

"Wait!"

The lack of response to his cautionary words stung the General as he looked out at the resistors. They stood perfectly still, resolute, and now, defiant.

"Very well."

The U.S. soldiers shouldered their firearms and took aim. The Resistance soldiers had stopped trying to force back the mob; there was no longer any need as they now all stood in stunned silence, watching with a mixture of triumph and horror.

"Don't! Stop!" DV-8 called out as 10-CC continued to race across the roof. She reached the edge, fully intending to continue in her attempt to escape the despair closing in around her. At the last moment she halted and peered down at the scene unfolding in the courtyard. The sight of the resistors, all lined up in their party uniforms, reminded her how things were before. It looked just like how they would line up to watch the weekly reports back when things made sense, back when she was happy and safe. The familiarity of this sight was enough to drive the despair back and stop her in her tracks, at least for a moment.

DV-9 stood looking out of the panoramic window of Brien's office. The General barked into his megaphone, and his voice boomed across the courtyard: "ON MY SIGNAL!"

"Look what you've done! I told you he'd do it!"

"Didn't DV-8 sort it?" Brien called over from the large desk on which his feet rested as he reclined in his chair.

He was busy tapping away on one of the new 'phones' the U.S. soldiers had given to him. It was similar to the old electronic notebooks the party used, except this one also had a camera, a torch and pornography on it, which Brien found made them much harder to put down.

"No! And the General's men are…"

"I thought I told the General to stand down."

"Well, he isn't! Do something!"

DV-9 stopped, dumbfounded, unable to believe she could hear someone yawning, given the current situation. She turned around to see Brien with a hand covering his mouth, tapping away on his device.

"Well, at least it will get sorted. One way or another," he replied absent-mindedly.

"The Supreme Leader indeed," she snarled sarcastically, staring back at him with nothing but contempt in her eyes.

From her position between the two mobs, Jane saw the muzzles raise and heard the chambers load.

"No!" She buried her face in the chest of the nearest Resistance soldier.

"Move!" John 2 pushed his way through the mob, away from what was about to happen. AC-DC took a deep breath, closed his eyes, and resigned himself to whatever would happen next.

DV-8 approached 10-CC cautiously, joining her at the roof's edge. He peered over and looked down at the huge drop stretching out below. Suddenly a fanfare rang out across the city, and all the infoscreens lit up at once.

Everyone turned and looked up to watch in stunned silence as one.

- XVII -

EVER SINCE THE REVOLUTION, since her world had been turned upside down right up until that very moment, 10-CC had wanted nothing more than to see the Supreme Leader's face and hear his voice once more. Mere seconds earlier, she would have sworn that if she'd ever had the pleasure of watching a broadcast from the Supreme Leader again, she would be enraptured and unable to turn away. This was everything she had longed for; leadership restored, a reinstatement of safety and security, a return to normality – to how things should be.

But as the Supreme Leader's face filled the countless screens and his voice boomed out across the city, miraculously her attention was drawn to something else. From the corner of her eye, she noticed something about the man standing next to her, DV-8. She turned to look at him and confirmed that his lips were moving ever so slightly, almost imperceptibly; that he was indeed mouthing the words just before they were proclaimed on the infoscreen by the Supreme Leader. She frowned, confused, and watched him with growing curiosity as the broadcast continued:

My friends, I am deeply sorry for any hurt my absence may have caused. Please know that I share your pain in these confusing and troubling times. We are still all in this together, and I want you to know that what you feel, I feel. What you think, I think. And what you do, I do…

These words punctured 10-CC's confusion and managed to break through to her. They seemed vaguely familiar, and she wondered where she had heard them before. She stared closely at DV-8 as she pondered them:

Please believe me, my friends, when I tell you that I have not brought all of this upon you lightly. Over the years, I have seen many lose their way and succumb to deviance. After a while, I believed everyone was the same and would eventually succumb without strict rules and regulations. I thought you, my friends, were like the rest, but now I see you are so much more…

10-CC's expression softened as she watched DV-8's lips silently forming these words. Her gaze was drawn to the rip in the knee of his overalls. She noticed it had reopened and was now only half stitched together. She smiled.

You have passed the test, my friends and proved that you no longer need my guidance or leadership to stay true. More importantly, you have proved this to yourselves. And this is all the more important now as I'm afraid I have to tell you that you must continue without me…

She resumed facing the screen but didn't hear another word. Her mind was racing, but no longer aimlessly through the never-ending darkness. Her thoughts had broken out into the light and were moving towards something. The Supreme Leader went on, regardless of her apathy:

Do not weep for me; two hundred and fifty-six years is a bloody good innings by anyone's count. I implore you, my friends, to look for the purpose, safety and love you found in me, in yourselves and one another...

DV-8, meanwhile, hadn't taken his eyes off the screen. He, too, found the reaction of the person standing next to him much more fascinating than the broadcast itself but dared not turn to look and find out what it was.

As for the others, those still troubled by deviance, you must allow them to come to peace in their own time and in their own way. No more reporting or controlling; focus on yourselves, and all will be well over time. After all, remember one of my most famous, insightful, and original sayings, 'be the change you want to see in the world.'

He knew the broadcast was almost over and continued to silently, robotically mouth the words to distract himself and avoid speculating on what might happen next.

And though we will not meet again in this lifetime, we shall meet in the place where there is no light. Goodbye, my friends, and good luck.

The image of the Supreme Leader dissolved, and the infoscreens cut to black.

Forever.

The noise from below was hard to discern. There was no sound of gunshots, but regardless, there was a strong reaction from both crowds: a collective human cry that was joyous and anguished and everything in between all at once.

DV-8 and 10-CC looked down into the courtyard. It was hard to make out precisely what was happening, but they could see the colours that had been so rigidly separated start to blend and move together. The white uniforms passed through the dull-green uniforms, and the multi-coloured group passed through the rigid line of black uniforms until there was no separation at all, just one large, multi-coloured crowd of people that was no longer so tightly packed but beginning to disperse in all different directions. The sweltering April breeze soon carried any noise away. DV-8 and 10-CC found themselves engulfed by an unusual calm. She noticed he was wiping something off his face from just under his left eye. Puzzled, she looked up into the sky.

"Is it raining, brother?"

"No."

He glanced from the dizzying drop below to 10-CC. Still standing at the edge of the roof, she peered over it. He went to speak but faltered. He realised that the panoramic view of the city spread out before him was what he had longed all his life to see from an office high up in the party HQ as an

Upper Party member. He scanned the scene, took a deep breath, and tried to appreciate something he had so long wished for so, but the ashen grey walls of the once brilliantly white buildings made this difficult. Then something peculiar caught his eye. The party HQ building towered high above every other building in the city except for one hulking apartment complex just a few miles away, which was as tall as the party HQ building itself, save for the flagpole. His confounding 'freedom of thought' was once again leading him to purposeless wondering, and for the first time, he didn't mind it. He was glad of the distraction. He recognised that he was seeking something to occupy his mind, which was now primarily concerned with 10-CC and what she might do next. His speculations filled him with dread, but he knew that he had to let her do whatever she wanted, whatever that meant.

They looked to the infoscreen on the side of the enormous apartment building across from them, as they had a thousand times before when seeking guidance for the future. With the screen blank, all they could see was the deep, black sheen of the glass surface reflecting the whole city, stretched out behind them, all the way back to the perimeter wall and even slightly beyond. They stared up into it, unflinching. For some unknown reason, DV-8 suddenly became conscious once again that they were standing close enough that their hands could reach out and touch. Her hand flickered to life and moved slowly towards his.

Dave reciprocated in kind.

THE END

HISTORICAL NOTES ON
DAVE'S NEW WORLD

Being a partial transcript of the proceedings of the Twelfth Symposium on 48th Century studies, held as part of the International Historical Association Convention, which took place on April 04, 5195.

Chair: *Professor Zamyatin, Head of the International Historical Association.*

Keynote Speaker: *Professor Bokanovsky, Director: Forty-seventh and Forty-eighth Century Archives, Oxbridge University.*

ZAMYATIN:

I want to welcome you all here and thank you for staying late for this talk following the main programme of lectures for the day. I can't say I am surprised at the low turnout for Professor Bokanovsky's talk, given the subject matter, and indeed this is why we scheduled the lecture after most attendees had left for the day. We at the International Historical Association believe that this is a fascinating period of human history which warrants further study, but we accept that the text being discussed was not the most important or insightful or indeed popular document of its time. Ultimately, it remains an obscure, curious footnote in the literary canon of the time, but we did commit to covering all aspects and documentation of the period during the Symposium.

If you could please bear with us, we will try to get this one over with as quickly as possible.

But before we proceed, a few announcements. The second UK civil war re-enactment commemorating The Battle of the Watford Gap in the mid-21st century, is cancelled. Apologies, we had thought scheduling the Symposium at the height of Summer meant all activities would be able to go ahead, but the bad weather has taken us all by surprise. Whoever heard of showers in April?

I also remind our keynote speaker to keep the talk brief, as many of us are tired and keen to get home. Professor Bokanovsky scarcely needs any introduction. He is notorious in historical academia for making bold, often unfounded claims, many of which have been widely discredited but are often very entertaining, nonetheless. Also, we couldn't find anyone else who wanted to talk about this particular title. His talk is part of the series Dictatorships and Despots: Lessons from Letters. The title being discussed today is 'Dave's New World'. With that, I ask that you try and give your full attention to the speaker and help me in welcoming him to the stage.

Professor Bokanovsky.
Muted applause.

BOKANOVSKY:

Thank you, Professor Zamyatin. As the title of my series of lectures implies, I wish to consider the lessons we can learn from historical documents and what they can teach us about the dangers of fascism so that we might avoid such mistakes in our own time. Today we will be discussing a niche, not very well-known, so-called manuscript, *Dave's New World.*

When it was first discovered, the manuscript bore no title. The moniker *'Dave's New World'* was appended to it later. It's not known who attributed the new title to the text, but research has shown it is some reference to a much older text from the mediaeval period, which has since been lost. A homage, or pun, so to speak, which was common in writings prior to the fourth enlightenment but which we would today accurately identify simply as plagiarism. It's even thought the title is supposed to be what used to be called a 'joke', which just goes to show you what passed for humour pre-fourth enlightenment!

It was not difficult to authenticate the existence of the principal players in the story or confirm that the events depicted were accurate owing to the excellent organisational skills and extensive record keeping of the government of the time known only as 'The Party'. The extensive surveillance they subjected their citizens to, while obviously slightly invasive, did mean there was plenty of corroborating video footage to cross-reference with the narrative and assess and affirm its authenticity. I must admit this made my job a lot easier, and for this, I must thank them. To The Party. *(Raises his glass. Drinks. Calls for a refill.)*

It was much more difficult, however, to ascertain the veracity of any of the facts surrounding the so-called 'U.S.' the government that supposedly gave aid to The Resistance, or to confirm the existence of any of the people mentioned who came from there, including the character referred to simply as, 'The General'.

While we have seen mention of the 'U.S.' in other historical documents, writings and diaries, their actions, characters, and temperaments seem so far-fetched, hypocritical, and draconian that most scholars agree the country is probably a fictitious, satirical invention of fiction. An amalgam, if you will, of any and all examples of abuses of power from around the world put together and used by writers of the time as a sort of shorthand to signify a corrupt government or deceitful leadership as their portrayals in such documents seem too ludicrous for them to have actually existed. We have been even less successful in finding out any information on what happened to our principal players after the events described in the manuscript. Did our protagonist thrive in the post-party world? Did his companion survive long after the story's conclusion, or did she elect to jump from the roof of the party headquarters? Did they end up together and live happily ever after? All of this we shall never know. I understand that some people find this a very unsatisfying resolution to the story, an insult even after giving up so much of their time to read it. I share their frustrations and question the author's decision not to pursue the narrative further. *(Hiccups.)*

As I have been asked to keep this talk brief, I will get right to the point; there is almost nothing new we can learn from Dave's New World that has not been expressed more artfully in other works or that we have not already figured out for ourselves. Any possible lessons relating to democracy, equality, or governance we now all believe anyway and practice inherently as part of our more advanced society, possibly even more advanced species by this point. Dave's New World is by no means the first work to warn about the dangers of totalitarianism, and with such an extensive reading list from history, as we now have, it would be almost impossible for us not to have gotten the message by now.

Following the Fourth and, God willing, final enlightenment, we no longer mindlessly and endlessly repeat the mistakes of the past as our ancestors did. We know the dangers of totalitarian regimes and how to guard against them. With or without texts like Dave's New World, we will never again allow undemocratic, authoritarian, fascist regimes to take hold, and we understand the importance of always being able to hold to account and question those in authority.

Muted applause. One audience member raises their hand.

I'm afraid we won't be taking any questions.

Luke Richards is a comedian and author living in London. Find him on Instagram: @Lukerichardscomedy